Author information

"Ash" Wragg retired from his "other life"
career, that included scientific writing, in 2010.
Since then he has contributed to the monthly
journal at his retirement community. As a
resident of that retirement community in south
eastern Pennsylvania for many years, he has
gathered together many humorous stories and
speculations that have led to the writing of this
novel. Everyone living in a retirement
community will recognize a bit of themselves in
this comedic work and they will understand
why Mr. Wragg has written it using a pen name.

D1311016

In appreciation

I would like to thank the friends and neighbors who have helped by offering good and hilarious suggestions and/or have edited this text. I provide only their initials to protect these good people from possible guilt by association. They are: KT, Cl, SW, JK, PP, AP.

Publishing rights

ISBN-13: 978-1974500499

ISBN-10: 1974500497

Book and eBook distribution through Amazon.com and Amazon Europe

HIPPIES INVADE
TODDLE MANOR!

Can west coast hippies live with
east coast seniors?

by

ASHTON WRAGG

A Novel

Description:

Two hippies, Uki and Shanti, leave California to avoid probable financial and legal problems with Uki's real-estate and hedge fund dealings. They move to Mexico until things quiet down and to await the next big thing. Billionaire Kingsley Conn contracts Uki to set up local markets for marijuana sales in any US state that has not legalized its sale and to assist in lobbying. Uki and Shanti choose Pennsylvania! If that is not strange enough, they decide to move into Toddle Manor, a conservative continuing care retirement community (CCRC) near Philadelphia. The current residents are not happy having their lives disrupted by intrusive style, hippy dress, loud rock and roll music, nude forest walks and vegetarian meals. Residents' plans to remove the hippies and owner/operator, Mr. Toddle's, efforts at reconciliation are outmaneuvered by Uki at every turn. See how these cultural clashes evolve and the mysteries unfold.

Dedication:

To my loving wife, to whom I have been married for as long as I can remember. A woman of such wisdom, integrity and insight that she has refused to have anything to do with this work from its inception.

PROLOGUE

Toddle Manor, a free-standing continuing care retirement community (CCRC), had been a grand 250-acre family estate in Sylvania County among the rolling hills of Penn's green woods in southeastern Pennsylvania. Beautifully renovated for group living, this majestic, two storied, redbrick, Georgian colonial manor attracted the financially more advantaged of the region. Residents live quiet orderly lives in their "Shangri-La." The Great Recession of 2007- 2009 caused the local senior citizens, usually ready to move into CCRCs, to stay put and wait out their lowered home values before selling. Now the Manor's occupancy is below the break-even threshold and it is in deficit spending.

Norbert Toddle III, owner and operator of the Manor, was searching for new revenue sources. He decided to reach out to the city of Philadelphia and to other less affluent areas for potential residents. Toddle calculated that by providing reduced entrance fees and filling apartments, the monthly maintenance fees would contribute enough income to operate in the black. To that end he wrote a letter to the editor of the American Organization of Continuing Care Retirement Communities' monthly bulletin touting his desire to see cultural diversity in senior living communities.

He sent a copy to the region's Daily Chronicle and to the Philadelphia Inquirer newspaper. Norbert Toddle and the Manor residents are in for a surprise. "Be careful what you wish for."

CHAPTER 1   SHANGRI-LA INVADED

"Have you two seen the new couple who just moved in?"

"No, what are they like, Gladys?" asked Martha.

"Well, they say you can't tell a book by its cover, but pony tail, loud voice, loud shirt, shorts and sandals and a wife with a bare midriff tells me a great deal! Mercy. Pass the butter, Mary Lou."

"They can't be new residents. They have to be visiting someone," whispered Mary Lou looking over her shoulder at the newcomers and spilling the butter pats into her Waldorf salad.

"Well, Charles and Eleanor Werthen are their greeters, and he introduced them to me. They are moving into Katherine Potter's old apartment."

"What are their names?"

"Asian sounding but they don't look it. Her name is Shanti."

"Shanti, what kind of name is that?"

"Well, Martha, it's hers, and do you know what they were saying to Charles when I met them this afternoon? They were wishing that there were 4-bedroom apartments. They don't know what they

are going to do with their surround sound entertainment center and the 3-D HD TVs."

"What are HR and those other initials?"

"It's HD not HR – stands for 'huge difference.' Don't you ever talk to your children? They know about all these things. It's all very expensive, makes a lot of noise and makes things so real that you want to hide."

"Gladys, you are making me so nervous; I may not be able to eat the homemade apple dumpling for desert I had so planned for and we don't get it very often."

"Oh, Mary Lou, order it anyway. If you really can't eat it, take it home with you for later. Don't you have that plastic bag in your purse?"

"Yes, a marvelous idea. That is just what I'll do. My, I feel better already, and I am just going to forget all about those people and hope that this is all a nightmare."

"Well wake up, friends. See for yourselves. Here they come with Charles and Eleanor. Pretty late to be arriving for dinner I should say. Look at the outfits - the dress code is right out the window! Gracious, what is Charles thinking of? I will be talking to him soon enough about this! I'm shocked that Eleanor would be seen with them," grumbled Gladys.

"My stars. Pony tail, shorts, sandals - that shirt is open down nearly to his belt and no jacket. Oh, goodness, look at her! That muumuu is practically see through! Are those tattoos? That is the end," exclaimed Martha."

Mary Lou said, "I am feeling faint. Where's my water." Her eyes became a bit glassy as her head slowly slumped forward toward the remains of her creamed chipped beef over wild rice, but she managed to catch herself. Straightening, she looked around embarrassed. Fortunately, no one had noticed. Every eye in the dining room was on the newcomers as they breezed in laughing and talking loudly shattering the orderly decorum of clicking silverware and periodic demure coughs and sneezes.

"The dress code for the dining room is jacket and tie during the winter and jacket without a tie in the summer," Charles tactfully mentioned.

"Shanti and me, we don't do rules. We're about

freedom. That's what the 60's was about. Pick our own path. If it feels natural and good, do it. Rules are sooo yesterday. Get real, Les!" said Suzuki loudly enough to create a chorus of sharp inhalations, four coughs, and astonished eyes at tables # 31 through #59.

"It's Charles, not Les. Ah yes, quite an interesting but highly controversial thought," said Charles hardly hearing Eleanor's stifled moan, as he threaded his way to table #70 avoiding the stares of the residents of good standing at tables #47 through #68.

"Good evening, Charles," came from table #58.

"Oh, hello Bill, Mary, Arnold, Allison," Charles answered without looking up from the floor or slowing the pace to introduce the new couple.

Hello Eleanor, that's a nice outfit you have on this evening," complimented table # 67.

"Oh, thank you Grace, I'll talk to you later," said Eleanor, bringing up the rear. She settled into the chair where Charles stood ready to assist in her seating.

"This is really early for dinner. Seven is better for tranquil digestion," offered Shanti as she flowed ethereally into her seat. "Nice dining room. Being served, that's cool."

Eleanor looked at the menu, but she was too deep into self-doubt to see it. *I know that it was not my fault that our rotation as "welcome greeters" for the 2nd floor of the Washington wing came up this week or that the Tanaka's moved onto our floor today,* she thought. *I feel as guilty as the day I skipped class in the 8th grade to watch Huck Reilly play football for Jeffersonville High. God probably has forgiven me for that but absolutely no one at Toddle Manor will forgive me for welcoming these people, but here I am, stuck with it. I could have had a headache, stayed in the apartment, made do with a toasted cheese sandwich and Chamomile tea, and read the Jeffersonville Historical Society News that has just arrived but I have never had a headache in my life and surely would have botched the whole thing. Besides, I have stood by Charles in every crisis for 51 years of marriage and that is the way it will stay, no matter what befalls me.*

Once seated, Charles, with his usual professorially worded and grammatically correct clarity, dove right into accurately establishing name, rank and serial number. "We met so briefly as you were moving in this afternoon that I am not sure that I caught your names. Therefore, to repeat, I am Charles Werthen and this is my wife, Eleanor. Being your greeters …"

"Huge 'hey' back, Les, Nor. Thanks for the big hello. Cool. I'm Uki, and this is Shanti. I call her Te." Shanti gently touched Charles and

Eleanor's arms. Slowly angling her head with closed eyes and with a smile of peace, as she passed Chi on to them.

Charles stared blankly and reviewed. His hearing was still reasonably good. Yes, he had said, "Uki," and yes, he had said, "Te."Since verification is at the heart of propriety, Charles said, "Pardon me, did I hear you say, 'Uki and, and Te'?"

"Right on, Les."

Briefly Charles looked first at Eleanor, her paleness now fading to gray, then to his right and left. There was no one within 6 feet of their table. Charles hesitantly inquired, "Les? Nor?"

"Love, cool get-to-know-ya' names. Cuts out the BS –starts comfort."

"But those are *not* our names," Charles quickly responded.

"That's ok, they should be. You need to be laid back. Too tight too long." Uki said, shaking his head. "You two gotta relax. I can feel the tension. Can't you, Te?"

Shanti, eyes closed, palms open upwards, softly said "Lover, intense. All over the room. Major

13

high frequency vibes. Chi is blocked. There's so much to do here freeing the stagnation. Kumbaya."

CHAPTER 2   DINNER and BEYOND

"Hi, I'm Mystie with a "y and ie" pointing to her slightly crooked name tag. I'll be your server tonight. What'll you guys have? Specials are meat loaf, quiche Lorraine, fish du jour, angel hair pasta with meat sauce."

Looking at the menu Shanti noted, "There are no green vegetables, just root vegetables and corn." In the 30 years in California she had never had red meat or a meal without greens.

"Well, there are other choices I am sure. What would you rather have?" offered Eleanor.

"Fresh asparagus tips lightly seasoned and boiled for 10 seconds would be nice. It's in season."

Uki added, "Te and me are vegetarians; we gave up the toxic stuff. What about you, Les and Nor?"

"Charles and Eleanor, if you don't mind," Charles sniffed, cocking an eyebrow.

Shanti continued, "What is the fish tonight?"

"Du jour," answered Mystie confidently.

"I meant, what *is* the fish du jour."

"It looks sorta white and smells pretty fishy. Most people have sent it back. I'd try something else if I were you. The meat loaf and brown gravy is always good."

"Would you please ask the chef to come out, dear?" asked Shanti.

"You mean Bud? Okay but don't hold your breath," replied Mystie as she trudged back toward the kitchen.

Charles carried on the interrogation. "Being your greeters means that we will arrange for you to have dinner partners for each evening through this week. We will attempt to provide you with answers to such salient questions that may arise during your acclimatization to Toddle Manor. First, what exactly are your names? Surely they're not Uki and Shanti."

"Yeah, Uki, that's for my first good bike – Suzuki before the Harley. Te? It's short for

Shanti – means blessed calm, rest, bliss –where you wanna be. Cool."

"Tanaka sounds Asian, but neither of you appears to stem from that heritage."

"We gave up on parents, their names, their rules, their chains – ancient history. Tanaka is a common Japanese family name in California. Good for business. Was in finance and real estate – 'lot of money there - a lot."

"Would you expound further? You are from California, we understand. How did you meet?"

"Came back from California for Woodstock, 1969. When time began."

"It is a long way from Woodstock to California! When and where did you marry?"

"Guess we've been together ever since we met at Woodstock." Uki replied.

Mystie interrupted, "He says he's too busy to come out - whacha want?"

Eleanor answered first, eager to change the subject, "I suggest speaking to the culinary director tomorrow during the day. His name is Jeff, Jeff Stuffsom. He tries to accommodate special health needs; I know he will be able to assist you." Eleanor was finding it hard to keep her mind off the deeply open chartreuse silk shirt and the massive gold chain that covered some of Suzuki's shaven chest. Speaking helped to pull her out of the state of shock that had frozen her larynx until that moment.

"Can I take you guys' orders now?" Mystie asked.

Shanti said softly, "Free-range organic chicken breast, asparagus tips, fresh fruit on spinach leaves and soy pita bread."

"Somethin' to drink?"

"Yes, love, green tea."

"The tea looks brown," Mystie cautioned

"Would you please ask the chef if he has green tea? If not, bottled water will have to do," responded Shanti with a sigh.

After hearing this interchange, Uki said, "Ditto. But I can tell ya' we'll change the

menu here to a healthy one soon. You folks can't keep eatin' this poison!"

After Charles and Eleanor ordered their meals, Eleanor soldiered on. Looking across the table at Charles to avoid Suzuki's chest on her right, "The greeter's card that marketing provided for us states, 'Mr. and Mrs. Tanaka, Suzuki and Shanti', is that correct? This will be going into the telephone directory."

"Sorry, no pita bread, no soy, no nothin'

organic. Bud says order from the menu or eat at the American Café," apologized Mystie. "How 'bout I get both you guys the fresh fruit platter, plain yogurt, chicken breast and water? "

"Okay Mystie, do that but not cool. Thanks for tryin'," Uki replied.

Doggedly persisting, Charles replayed the conversation, "So then you two met at Woodstock, were married and moved to California sometime after that."

"Somethin' like that, " Uki replied. "We were in the protest movement, livin' in an ol' VW bus. But bein' broke and hungry gets ya' thinkin.' Seemed like investment banking had a better future than the peace movement."

"Mr. Tanaka, somewhere along the line you both elected to change your names. Quite novel. Of course, that would have been quite inconceivable for us."

"Just Uki, friend. Life's too short for formal. We like bein' comfortable and cool. Life is good this way. You guys, we'll help ya' but ya' really gotta loosen up. You're so generation. It'll kill ya'. Les 'n Nor is a good start for gettin' you away from middleclass zipped-up, buttoned-down. Let go and get deep into your senses. With some real effort, bet ya' could turn out to be really nice people."

With elegant control, Eleanor speaking through her teeth slowly and firmly proclaimed, "Charles and I thoroughly enjoy our names and our lives just as they are. We are quite content."

"You feel that way now, but Uki and I will help you unlock deep richness, inner warmth, love - the true sensuality and passion of your inner selves. There is a joyful world inside and out. It is natural. The universe is waiting for you to repel your gravity-bound karma and rise to join the path, to become joyful free spirits," soothed Shanti.

"Really, I don't believe we are looking for passion!" Eleanor quipped. "What do you like to do? Do you have hobbies? Are you looking for a local church?"

"Meditate outdoors, yoga, Tai Chi, being into nature, chanting in drum circles, making love, reading poetry, and taking long nature walks," Shanti replied.

"We're naturists, ya' know; our spirits resonate with all of nature," Uki responded. "We start the morning communin' with nature's spirits touching ours in our natural state. We hear the trees growin', the birds flyin' and we know they hear us. And of course, weed, sex and rock and roll."

Eleanor's pallor and Charles' flush deepened.

Their forks paused in midair as they imagined the negative impact this couple could have on Toddle Manor. Charles cleared his throat, "You don't mean that you actually walk about out of doors in the nude, do you?"

"That's the basic condition of all nature including humans. We're not born with clothes on. To feel the closeness of nature, you have to be part of it, Les," Uki explained quietly. "Clothes are part of the chains of society. You should have been at Woodstock with us, 500,000 mostly nude, stoned natural hippies. It was beautiful even with the rain and mud. Your lives would've been changed forever like ours was."

"Well I'm sure you're right about that! However, I can't envision that being for the better. Do understand that we are a conservative people here in the East and at Toddle Manor. It is a very comfortable, predictable life with many friends and enjoyable days. It is our 'Shangri-La.' If you walk around here, or anywhere in the East, in the nude you will be arrested!" Charles huffed, leaning forward across the table to emphasize his point."

Uki leaned back smiling, "Hey, Les, chill. Ya' can't do that in California either, least not yet. There are designated places and ya' can do it at home. It's a lifestyle like any other. I bet there are many designated places right around here.

We don't go in fer the international nudists'
day, nude gardening day, nude bicycling day,
nude parade day. We keep a low profile."

"Whatever brought you both east to the
Philadelphia area for retirement?"

"California - been there, done that. Time for a
change. We're both born in the East. This
seems like a nice area fer retirement; s'pose it's
better than most."

After dinner, Charles and Eleanor attempted to
continue the obligatory orientation.

"Les, look, you two don't have ta' walk us
around this place. We had a tour last month
when we signed up ta' come in here. I don't
think much has changed since then. Te and me
gotta unpack just ta' go ta' bed tonight. Ask you
a couple of questions, then let's knock off."

"It's Charles, Suzuki. That is quite satisfactory
with us, I'm sure."

"Do you have Tai Chi and meditation groups or
do we have to start them?"

"As for group exercises, there is a 9 AM walking
group on Tuesdays lead by our trainer, Wanda
Thump. Some residents seem to enjoy it, if you
like that sort of thing," offered Eleanor.

How do we meet up with the food service director so we can get a good vegetarian menu here?"

"As for meeting with the culinary director, I suggest you talk to Rhonda at the main reception desk tomorrow. She will be in at 8:30 AM. She can arrange a meeting for you with Jeff Suffsom."

Shanti and Uki looked at each other and turned. "Night, Les and Nor." They headed across the ornate, mahogany wainscoted Great Hall towards the Washington wing stairs up to No. 223 and the moving boxes. The rear view of Shanti's semitransparent muumuu and Suzuki's shorts and sandals provided one last chilling nightcap for the Werthens. "It's Charles and Eleanor, and yes, good night," replied Charles. After watching them disappear up the stairs,

Eleanor broke the silence, "Charles, do you really think they intend to live here permanently?"

"Hope is the last thing to die, Eleanor. We can keep hoping that this is all a big mistake that soon will be rectified. Let's walk outside and get some fresh air. I see Gladys, Martha and Mary Louise bearing down on us."

CHAPTER 3 THE MORNING AFTER

If no interesting gossip comes up by the end of breakfast, it is customary to start a rumor of your own. At breakfast this morning there was no need of that. Uki and Shanti were on everyone's lips. Eleanor and Charles' table was surrounded by indignant and/or titillated residents. Charles stood, asked for quiet and evenly stated, "To date all we know is that their names are Suzuki and Shanti Tanaka, that they are not Japanese despite their surname, that they met at the 1969 Woodstock Festival, and that they moved to California where we presume they have lived until moving here to Toddle Manor yesterday. We have no details as to exactly where they lived in California. They were both born some-where in the East and have decided to retire here as well. They are vegetarians. He was involved in finance and real estate. She has led yoga and meditation groups, nature walks and enjoys planning and creating vegetarian cuisine.

"I am sure we will all learn more as time goes on. Although the subject is ripe for exaggeration and rumor, I respectfully request that you resist this temptation and restrict yourself to the facts as I have just stated them. There is no value in interrupting breakfast with further questioning as we have no other information to relate. If you would kindly return to your tables and resume breakfast, we will wish you all a good morning." He had not brought up the apparent aversion to rules and dress code. The latter had already been noted widely throughout the dining room the night before. The business about being "naturists," Charles and Eleanor felt might best remain undisclosed for the present.

The last two ladies leaving the Morning Room were heard to say, "So they are Japanese - must have come over on a ship. They landed in California and they sold wood stocks, whatever they are, to real-estate people for a living. I must say their English is fairly clear from what I hear."

After breakfast, on the way back to their apartment, Eleanor suggested stopping by the Tanaka's apartment. There was no answer at the door so they moved on down the hall but turned back when they heard the door open. Coming back, they stop short. Eleanor stifled an, "Oh" as Shanti stood in the doorway covered by a small towel from mid-bust to upper thigh.

"Peace and good morning dear people. Would you like to come in? I was just finishing my morning meditation," smiled Shanti.

"No, no!" Charles and Eleanor simultaneously declared. "We're so sorry to have disturbed you in your, ah, meditation,"

Charles said as they turned and briskly retreated down the hallway. Fumbling with the keys to their apartment more than usual, Charles finally opened the door. They entered quickly, closed the door and he leaned against it. Turning to each other and with one voice they moaned, "Good Lord."

Meanwhile Uki had finished his meditation and was dressed in shorts and a T-shirt emblazoned with LOVE NOW! On the back of it was a large green bush with two pairs of protruding ankles and feet, one pair pointing up and the other pointing down. He was out to explore the vast expanse of the south lawn at the rear of the Manor. Finding a path half way down on his right, he entered a densely-wooded area with underbrush and a high canopy of mixed tulip poplar, pin oak, and sycamore. There were several deer paths, and he followed one deep into the woods. Deliberately looking for heavy thicket, he worked his way through brambles of blackberry bushes. There he came upon a sundrenched opening in the trees. He fixed these coordinates in his GPS, and retraced his steps to the lawn and turned down the slope to the lower parking lot behind the old stables. There he unlocked the side door of his large black trailer and climbed in. A few minutes later, he peered out of the rear trailer door then cautiously emerged with a bucket, a canvas bag and a spade. He walked briskly 20 yards across the lawn to the near edge of the woods and disappeared into its shadows

Shanti's appointment with Jeff Stuffsom was at 10:00 A.M. in the culinary director's office. Breezing in through the open door, Shanti smiled, "Peace, Jeff, my name is Shanti. I am excited to meet you. Why didn't Eleanor tell me you were sooo handsome?" The long flowing blonde hair, the tall willowy figure in a powder blue halter and skin toned yoga pants paralyzed Stuffsom's vocal cords.

"Glorblk, ghaaah, gool margeen (cough). Come, come in, please. Haaave a seat, Mrs. Shanti."

"Just Shanti, love. We just moved in yesterday, and I wanted to meet with you right away."

"Really!", Jeff croaked. "How come, aaaaah, Shanti?"

"Jeff, you're the master here. I can tell you've been wanting to expand your dietary selections for a long time. Let's work really closely together; I mean work *really closely* on a vegetarian diet so everyone here can live a better life - one filled with energy, vitality and passion. You know what I mean?"

Wiping his moist brow with the sleeve of his white shirt, "Well I mean I can't really do *anything* I want, but we certainly could look at a vegetarian selection or two if we have a call for it."

"What would I need to do to convince you that we need a daily vegetarian menu here now?" Shanti ask as she leaned over the desk toward Jeff.

Looking up from Shanti's cleavage to her deep blue eyes, Jeff chirped, "Why don't I put together some vegetarian suggestions. I can leave them in your mailbox and you can let me know what you think. Do you have any particular favorites?"

Still leaning over the desk and looking down into Jeff's eyes, Shanti opened her lips slightly and softly said, "Asparagus - fresh asparagus, fresh fruit, green salads, soy pita bread, green tea, wild fish and organic free-range chicken." As she slowly rose, Shanti placed her hand on Jeff's forearm, "I can feel your energy. You have good karma. That is good, very good. I am so looking forward to your getting in touch with me." She exited like a vapor leaving Jeff speechless, motionless, suspended.

CHAPTER 4   TAI CHI. HIDDEN TREASURE

"Mary Lou, where are you going," asked Gladys from behind dark glasses?

"Oh, I'm heading off to the Tai Chi exercises on the south lawn. It starts at 10:30, and I just have time to get there. Are you coming? It should be good for us."

"Well I don't need you telling me what is good for me! You are the one who needs reminders. I don't think you should be doing this sort of gibberish. You're not really going to encourage *that* woman, are you? Gracious! I saw the announcement on the bulletin board in the mailroom with all those strange names on it. The only one I understood was 'meditation.' The others do not sound very Christian to me!"

"Oh Gladys, it's all about relaxation and balance – tranquility and peace of mind." replied Mary Lou still walking towards the French doors exiting the Great Hall to the south lawn.

"Martha, and where have you been? I thought you were right behind me coming

out from breakfast."

"I stopped by the mailroom. Did you see the

announcement on the bulletin board? There is a Tai Chi program on the south lawn at 10:30, a meditation group and then a healthy living seminar on vegetarian diets. Sounds very interesting. I want to observe, from a distance, for now."

"My stars," huffed Gladys, rolling her eyes and throwing up her arms. "Not you too! Mary Lou is actually going out there to do whatever this 'chi chi' is. I'm flabbergasted that you people can fall for such corruption. You two need to consolidate with me and put your energies into planning for a meeting with Mr. Toddle. "We have to get rid of this outrageous pair before they get settled in here. They don't belong here. They're not like us. We don't like them, and I doubt very much that they will like us. It's a total mismatch. I have no idea why they would want to come here in the first place, but that's their business. Our business is to have them leave and go somewhere else and let us return to the peace and quiet of our retirement. Well, I'm going to talk to Charles and Eleanor. You two do whatever you want. I'll talk to you at lunch about our plan of attack."

"Our Chi is flowing beautifully, wonderfully, smoothly. Our energy is flowing without obstruction. We are free; we are alive. Deep breath in - slowly. Hold it. Now breathe out slowly and hold it. Concentrate on the breath. Relax. Feel your muscles relax starting from your head. Let your tension flow slowly down, down, down your arms and off your fingertips.

Down your chest and stomach, down your legs and off your toes. Be in the moment. Think of the breath. Be timeless. Eternal peace. Breathe slowly." Shanti spoke softly as she led Mary Lou, four other women and one man seated in a circle about her.

Gladys marched across the Great Hall to the Washington wing staircase and up to the second floor. A blast of Mick Jagger's "I Can't Get No Satisfaction" caused her to rush down the hall, bent forward, holding her ears. Taking down one hand, she knocked on the Werthen's door. Charles answered promptly, "Gladys, come in and quickly." He closed the door. "It's much quieter in here. What happened? You're wearing sun glasses. Are those black eyes?"

"I went to see my lawyer about getting rid of these hippies. I had to use his rest room in the hall so I hung the long ribbon for the key around my neck. While I was bent over unlocking the door, some young thing in 5" red heels and a short red dress half way up her thigh jerked the door open from the inside and threw me in on the bathroom floor! It was a hit-and-run. I never saw her face. And stop smirking. It was not funny. Skinned both knees to boot! How can you stand that disgusting music?"

"We can't. We have arranged a meeting with Mr. Toddle for tomorrow. There has to be a change; this is intolerable. In the apartment, it's reasonably well controlled but we can't have the windows open or sit out on our balcony. That is really painful. And of course, the hallway..."

"Well that's the very reason I came up to talk to you and Eleanor. We have to get those people to leave. They are disrupting everything. That woman is cavorting out on the south lawn right now, and she's actually getting some residents to follow her lead. I can't believe it!" Why on earth would they want to come East, and of all places here, to torture us? Why didn't they just stay in California with the other crazies? Anyway, my lawyer said we need "solid evidence" before trying to evict those two so I am working on a plan to spy on them to get some evidence."

Charles turned and called into the bedroom, "Eleanor could you please come in here. We need to have a strategy session."

Uki finished the article he was writing in the apartment, turned off the music, came out of the apartment and headed for the Great Hall's French doors. He crossed the patio aiming for the old stables. It was a good leg stretch down the gentle slope. Forsythia was coming into bloom, and the willows had a light green halo. *Let's see what's behind these 10 large doors,* Uki thought. The right-hand door was unlocked. It opened. Closing it after him, Uki stood adjusting to the dim light coming through the dirty windows at the ends of the building.

He saw new and old maintenance equipment, two snow plows, a small truck, stacks of fencing, shovels and a lot of odds and ends jumbled in box stalls still present from a bygone era. As his eyes adjusted further, other things of interest appeared. Uki walked about slowly. After shuffling through old horse shoes, halters, brushes and broken bits of hardware, he saw the partial outline of a trap door in the far rear right-hand corner. Quickly scratching through the dust, dirt and grit, Uki outlined the entire door and the door ring. With some effort, he swung the large door up and latched the ring to its hook on the wall.

Peering down into the darkness as the dust cleared, Uki could see steep, rough wooden steps. His CZX7000 threw a bright light across the cement floor littered with broken flower pots, insulation, and scraps of building materials. The stairs creaked from disuse but held his weight. To his right was an exterior door with a small window looking onto the remote parking lot. Uki could see through the dirty pane. Outside large weathered timbers were stacked against the door. At the far end of the room was a slightly open door. Uki moved toward it cautiously stepping through the dust and debris. With great difficulty he managed to open the door wide enough to slide through as it groaned in protest. Inside was an old wood burning stove used to heat the long-gone stable hands' sleeping quarters above. In the shadows Uki stumbled into a pile of wood stacked high against the wall behind the stove.

It moved slightly. Shining his light down to the.floor, he noticed that the wood pile appeared to have moved as a solid piece. The edge had definitely come away from the wall. Getting his fingers behind the edge and with his foot against the wall, Uki pulled back the wood pile far enough to slip behind it. His cell phone's flash light was not bright enough to reach the limits of this large room. Uki searched and found a wall switch. Taking the cobwebs down and crossing his fingers, he threw the large lever. A double row of dim lights shone down from the ceiling. The room extended the full remaining length of the stable above.

"Awwwwwwwwwesome! Whada we got here?" Wiping off the thick layer of dust from a bottle, Uki read the label, "Canadian Club, blended Canadian whisky." One, two, three, four, five, six, seven, eight, nine, ten rows of full and four rows of empty tall narrow racks. One, two, three, four, five, six, seven shelves. How far do they extend? "Three feet to a pace," thought Uki as he counted, "One, two, three." And on and on he counted... "Twenty-four, twenty-five, twenty-six." That's 78 feet of bottles! Pulling out the CZX7000, he asked, "At current market prices converted from Canadian to US dollars, 0.75 liter bottles, 78 linear feet minus 4 feet for the vertical

stanchions, times 10 rows of racks,7 shelves each. How much whiskey is here and what is it worth?"

Three seconds passed then the phone texted, "5180 feet, 2.5 bottles per foot, 12,950 bottles. Current average bargain price $20.00 per bottle. Value of aging not calculated. At the average current exchange rate, converted to USD, total value is $259,000. Prohibition limited edition Gates bottle auction price - $61.00 not included." Uki dropped down onto a dusty wooden crate marked "Windsor, Ontario."

"If I drank a liter a day – no, could never make it," Uki wondered aloud. After ten minutes of muttering, smiling and head nodding, he rose and retraced his steps, turned off the light and closed the false wood pile door. Backing away using an old broom to scatter the dust obscuring his footprints on the floor, he climbed the stairs and closed the trap door- again brushing dirt over his foot prints. At the stable door, Uki cautiously peered out. Seeing no one, he slid out then turned around and down along the stable's foundation to the lower level. There he found the exterior door. Quietly removing the timbers overlaying it, he checked the old rusty padlock. A quick jerk opened it. Uki clamored down the 20-foot-long slope to the remote parking area, he unlocked the trailer and entered the rear door.

Reappearing and coming up the rise to the door in the stable's foundation, Uki re-moved the rusty lock and replaced it with his own sturdy camouflage colored padlock. Satisfied, Uki returned to and reentered the trailer, closed the door and sat down in his brown leather chair, deep in thought. Then a light in his eyes sparked a smile. Uki searched the CZX7000 directory and touched a name.

"Duer, Dodd, Dawson and Duer, may I help you?"

"I would like to set up a trust. Can you FAX me a standard trust form if I give you the trust name and the names of the trustees? Cool. The title is, 'Toddle Trust for Senior Enhancement.' The trustees are: Norbert A. Toddle and Uki – yes, u-k-i, Tanaka. Pur-pose: To provide wealth equivalents for the pursuit of enhancing senior living at Toddle Manor. One signatory only is needed to initiate a distribution or contract. I will be looking for your FAX and your bill and any special instructions for authentication. I will FAX back the completed forms and signatures. Thank you and good bye." Satisfied, Uki set up a ledger on the phone. Each bottle of Canadian Club ($20.00) will be designated as a "unit" to keep a level of privacy should anyone be nosing around in the future.

What a find! Sitting back, he envisioned how he would expend these "units" for business purposes. He had big plans to finance.

***

"Now we are in a state of peaceful awareness. Come let us do forest air breathing, shinrin-yoku." As she led her little band down the south lawn to the closest path entering the soft spring greenery to the deep woods beyond. Shanti softly crooned, "Follow along behind me – do what I do."

CHAPTER FIVE   UKI AND MR. TODDLE
DISCUSSION – INVITATION for KEY NOTE
ADDRESS

"You are so hot, I tingle every time I pass this desk," schmoozed Uki.

Rhonda looked up over her half-glasses, "Good morning, Mr. Tanaka."

"Uki, to you, sweet nectar."

"Off the record, may I say that you are so full of it that I should resent your approach. However, divorced, middle-aged, 15 pounds overweight and menopausal, I do not approve but don't stop. Who knows when I will ever hear it from a well-meaning gentleman? How can I assist you without getting fired?"

"Is Bert in?"

"Bert...!" coughed Rhonda. "Oh Lord, shhhhhh. Never say that. You had better clean up your act if you expect to talk to Mr. Toddle. He is a very formal gentleman and does not tolerate stepping outside of protocol." Toggling the intercom, "Ber..., ah, Mr. Toddle, Mr. Tanaka, one of our new residents is here. He wishes to have a brief meeting with you. I suggested that he schedule a future date, but..."

"It is all right, Rhonda. I have a few minutes. Send him in."

"Yes, Sir," Rhonda waved to the door behind her and nodded to Uki while sliding to her left to avoid Uki's right hand as it stretched toward her thigh as he passed. Winking and blowing her a kiss, Uki walked past the reception desk, depressed the heavy brass lever handle and opened the six-panel solid mahogany door to Mr. Toddle's private office. Rhonda sat back with a great sigh and thought, *Oh for those days again. What happened to romance? Leisurely dinners out with a charming gentleman toasting the evening with fine champagne. Now it's home alone to canned bean soup, saltines and a Coors light.*

Mr. Norbert Toddle III was standing behind his neat mahogany executive desk. With a tolerant smile and a rigidity born of being raised on "no" and "proper," he offered a

slight nod of recognition.

"Mr. Tanaka, it is good to see you. I trust that your move into Toddle Manor went smoothly and that all is in proper order. How may I be of assistance today, Sir?"

"Uki."

"I beg your pardon?"

"Uki, just Uki –that's cool."

"You wish me to address you as what?"

"Uki, man."

Dropping into the large burgundy leather chair beside a large window, Uki slouched back and enjoyed sinking slowly into the form-fitting back and seat cushions. "Whoa, ya' got mahogany everywhere - even the ceiling! So East Coast. Couldn't sell it in California. Me, I couldn't work in here. Couldn't breathe."

It was too early in the morning to permit being upset, although the occasion called for it. Mr. Toddle turned, gazed out the window behind his desk and slowly took a deep breath. Turning and with dignity seating himself in his black leather executive chair, he stared at Uki, "Toddle Manor's commitment to our residents is to respect and to maintain their dignity at all times. That includes my addressing all residents by their surnames. And 'Uki,' for whatever that is a contraction, does not qualify. Therefore, I shall address you as 'Mr. Tanaka.' Now then, how may I help you? I do have another appointment very shortly."

"Buried 'dignity' years ago, Bert, not cool. Uki –

yeah that has a cool feel -- laid back – it's me."

"Yes, yes, certainly we want you to feel comfortable and at home here. Toddle Manor is non-discriminatory and welcomes diversity, of course."

"Awesome, Bert, I have a proposition for you - how to upgrade this place so it's cool."

"Sir!" Norbert Adams Toddle III, grandson of the esteemed benefactor of the cultural arts, Republican state senator, and powerful sugar magnate, fairly screeched! Awed, Uki watched as Mr. Toddle's face turned brilliant red then faded to ash. Toddle's head started to drop forward but immediately jerked up with the resilience of generations of good breeding. Color crept back like a sunrise from beneath his white shirt collar. Focusing his eyes, they found Uki. Licking his lips, Mr. Toddle continued, "You may have a right to be called whatever you wish by your companions, but you do not have a right to offend others here, and that includes me! I wish to be addressed as 'Mr. Toddle' at all times. I hope that is quite clear. Now if you will excuse me..."

"Mr. Toddle, you have a long-distance call," Rhonda interrupted over the intercom.

"Who is it?" harrumphed Toddle.

"The president of, sounds like, 'ochra.'"

"Of what?"

Rhonda clicked off for ten seconds then back on, "The American Organization of Continuing Care Retirement Communities."

"I will take the call."

"Line 1."

"Good morning. This is Norbert Toddle. Yes, Mr. Rauheckler, a pleasure. Oh, 'Otto,' all right; just call me Norbert, ha ha. How may I be of service? Yes, yes, certainly. Yes, of course, I would be happy to assist in... Oh, I see. Well I am flattered and honored that you liked my Letter to the Editor on diversity. Key note speech at the national meeting here at the Convention Center? This is rather short notice, but I .... Oh, I see. He would have been very good. San Francisco, um, too far.

Yes, I understand. No offense taken. These things happen. Happy to oblige. Yes, then next Monday - a teleconference to coordinate everything. The key note date is? May 20th – the last day. A farewell reception at the Union League that evening? That will be nice. Yes, I am certain Drusilla will be able to accompany me and thank you for this invitation. Yes, thank you, ah, Otto. Yes, Goodbye."

Mr. Toddle, smiling like he had just sold 6 apartments, turned from the side window behind his desk, hung up the phone with a flourish, and was startled to see Tanaka. "I thought you had gone! Well I guess you heard that I have been asked to be the featured speaker for a special session on cultural diversity at our national meeting here in May. All the most prominent people in the industry will be there. Quite an honor! Quite."

Uki, still sitting in the chair by the window, nodded. "Awesome, Bert, even if you are just the local back up fer the real man. Let's go big time. Make a serious impression. I got just the wheels fer you and Silla."

Mr. Toddle, imagining himself at the podium as the packed hall applauds his presentation, glanced sideways at Uki, "Goodbye, Sir. Have a nice day."

Uki left with a shaka sign, "Hang loose."

Intercom chirped on. "Mr. Toddle, you are five minutes late for the special Resident Council Executive Committee meeting in the small conference room."

Norbert Toddle rose slowly, picked up his notes

from the corner of his desk and made for the door deep in thought. *This fellow, Uki, makes me uneasy. Something vaguely familiar about him. Who is he? Why did he and Mrs. Tanaka decide to come East? Of all the retirement facilities on the East Coast, why here – really? Why Toddle Manor? There are no other residents like them here. Do they have relatives in the area? What is the attraction? Are they hiding out?* Toddle made a mental note to search the internet for possible police records.

CHAPTER 6   THE ESCALATOR INCIDENT

Uki exited the inner office as Rhonda picked up the ringing telephone. "Good morning, Toddle Manor, Rhonda speaking, how may I help you?"

"This is Sylvania County Hospital Emergency Trauma Center. We have a resident of yours, a Mr. Earl Dar..., Darblasdt. He insists on leaving against medical advice. He has had head trauma. The laceration has been sutured, but he cannot be cleared for discharged until he has a CAT scan and medical clearance. Mr. Darblasdt insists that you send the bus for him immediately."

"I will transfer you to the medical department so you can discuss the issue with them. Under these circumstances, I am not authorized to send transport even if it were available."

Earl grabbed the phone from the nurse in the Trauma Center. "Rhonda is that you? Look, call Hal on your walkie-talkie and tell him to get the hell over here pronto. I'm not gonna sit around here with these nincompoops all day!"

"Mr. Darblasdt, please stop shouting," Rhonda asserted. "We cannot pick you up against doctor's advice. Now just relax and..."

"I'll 'relax' you when I get back. Now you get Hal on this damn phone, and I'll tell him what to do!'

Uki, walking by, could hear both ends of the conversation. "Let me talk to him," he said picking up the desk extension phone. "Earl, cool it. Listen up." Uki turned away from Rhonda and lowered his voice. "Brother, I feel your pain. Stay cool; sign yourself out and Uki will pick you up in 20 minutes. Look for a red Alfa Romeo convertible coupe – top down. Cool. Oh yeah, Earl, one more thing. If you die it's on you, right? Right. Bye." Uki hung up the phone. "Rhonda, woman, hang loose. Everything is totally K." He turned, walked back to the Great Hall, crossed it, went out the south French doors and walked briskly across the patio and down the lawn toward the enclosed garages at the edge of the remote parking lot.

It had started out as the usual bus trip to Smart Shopper, Earl recalled as he searched around for his clothes in the curtained ER unit. He wanted to be ready to get out of there as soon as this guy, Yukr or whoever, showed up in his sports car. Buses - he hated the help he needed getting on and off the bus. Errrrrr. But he needed socks and maybe a shirt if shirts were on sale. Hal had stowed Earl's walker below. Earl sat in the front seat just inside the bus door. "Where the hell is my other shoe?" he mumbled. He did not talk to the other residents on bus trips, and he did not want to hear any of their jibber-jabber and laughter.

46

Once the bus had bounced and jolted down Baltimore Pike, turned right into the mall and screeched to a stop in front of Smart Shopper, Earl was up and at the door. Earl got down with a minimal of grouching and resistance to Hal's helping hand. Once outside with his walker unfolded and ready to go, Earl pushed off without looking back. He had little patience with being slowed or obstructed in his path so he moved out ahead of the others residents. Barreling through the main door he grabbed the arm of a passing salesman, "Men's department?"

"Second floor, Sir, and remember to put the walker in the security rack on the left of the escalator."

"Stick it in your ear," Earl threw back over his shoulder as he sped off in the direction of the escalator. Although gauging the speed of the escalator steps progressively had become more challenging, Earl charged straight at them. The front two legs settled firmly on a step. As he ascended, the walker settled back and Earl alertly lifted the rear keeping it level. The exit at the second floor was equally well executed. A quick right turn and he was at men's shirts. "Hrumpf," Earl grumped dropping the price tag of a pin striped dress shirt. He moved on to socks. "Where do they get these prices?" he fumed. "After the War, I could get a dozen for the price of three of these and better quality too." He picked out a black three pack, paid cash and headed back to the escalator deciding to wait on the bus until it returned to the Manor.

Earl moved quickly onto the down escalator – too quickly. The walker surged forward before he had grasped its cross bar. Earl lunged foreword as the walker pitched down away from him. His low, penetrating yowl was quickly joined by the clatter of ricocheting aluminum against the stainless-steel side walls and the heavy thumping of a ponderous body as Earl and his walker somersaulted down the escalator steps and through women's wear. Earl ended up sprawled out, dazed and bleeding in bathrobes and nighties. The walker was totaled but recognizable in jewelry. He grimaced vaguely remembering lurching into a rack of lady's dresses, getting tangled up and going down again. What did happen after that? How did he get to the Emergency Room at Sylvania? He woke up slowly with his shirt and pants off, in a hospital gown, and a nurse was putting a cold compress on his forehead. The headache - yeah, ugh, the headache was still there.

Earl grabbed his bloodied shirt and pants, pulled back the curtain and limped to the exit doors. As he emerged onto the sidewalk he heard the revving of a powerful engine and the squealing of tires as the Alfa Romeo did a tight 180 in front of him.

"Earl. Peace, brother. Uki, to the rescue. Get

in. Don't get that bloody bandage on the headrest." Down shifting into 1st, he said, "Let's haul."

Earl, still in his hospital gown, fell into the right bucket seat feeling the welcoming warmth of the heated seat. Nice touch, he thought as he buckled his seat belt just in time to avoid pitching over into Uki's lap as the roadster turned sharply right and roared out of the ER circle. They squealed out the "in" drive as an orderly and nurse rushed out through the automatic sliding glass doors, chart in hand, waving furiously after Earl. Turning left against the light and double clutching into 2nd, then 3rd gear in quick succession, Uki opened up the Alfa Romeo as they escaped south on Baltimore Pike.

"Who the hell are you, the Lone Ranger?" shouted Earl over the engine and wind noise, holding his neck against the whiplash of gear shifts. "Are you the hippie I heard moved in with a sexy blond?"

"An angel of mercy, lifting the spirits of a weary world. Seeking nirvana. Give you a big high five for shooting the escalator. Reminds me of boogie boarding down the Big Sur cliff! Yeah, straight down. I was feeling no pain that day, no pain, until I hit bottom. Ugh, oh yeah! OK, Earl, 20 miles in 15 minutes – not bad. Could have done better except for the traffic." Down shifting through the sharp left turn between the stone pillars onto the Manor drive then rounding up over the cobblestone courtyard to the main entrance, the Alfa Romeo screeched to a stop. Earl unfastened his seat belt, grunted as he rolled his body up to a painful half stance. He waved over his shoulder at Uki as the roadster circled and headed out again.

Before reentering traffic on Baltimore Pike, he spoke into the CZX7000, "GPS. Destination. Capitol building, Harrisburg PA. Proceed on highlighted route. Local speed limit 45 mph. No marked police vehicles within 3.71 miles. Follow toll road for 75 miles. Rate changes frequent and currently not known. Historic data calculates your travel time at 62 minutes. Have a nice trip, Uki."

With the left hand, Earl grasped the nearby waist-high ornate trash receptacle for support and pushed it over to the heavy main door. He held his examination gown closed in the back and his bloody clothes with his right hand while pushing the front door auto-open pressure pad with his right elbow. Once inside, five painful steps to the left and he was in the cart storage alcove gingerly sitting down in his electric cart. He was in no mood to see or to be seen. His goal: a high-speed run to the apartment unseen. Having disconnected the speed governor for upcoming Senior Sports Day, Earl figured he had a 50/50 chance of making it. Exiting the cart alcove, Earl saw Zebedee Chaladon sitting on a high stool in his usual black polo shirt, black Khakis and black sandals. As Earl passed by, Zebedee's foreboding monotone reached out.

 "If you die tonight, where will you be tomorrow?"

"Go to hell," snarled Earl.

"Prophetic," Zebedee responded.

CHAPTER 7   THE EXECUTIVE COMMITTEE
MEETING

The Executive committee of the Residents'
Council was waiting for Mr. Toddle when he
arrived at the Willow Hollow conference room
on the first floor of the Madison building.
Stopping a moment to collect himself, he then
created, "the smile" and opened the door.
"Good morning everyone, my apologies for
being detained by a most important long-
distance telephone call. Now to the business of
the day. First there is the upcoming annual
Senior Sports Day, and we are the host
community. Although this event is completely
in your hands to arrange and produce from
soup to nuts, I would like to offer our complete
cooperation and any assistance the
maintenance and culinary departments might
supply. I, of course, will open the ceremonies
and also will hand out the prizes at the end of
the day. Are there any comments or
questions?"

"First, we will call the role for the record,"
Eleanor Werthen interrupted looking over her
half glasses at Mr. Toddle.

"Oh yes, of course. Excuse me for barging
ahead in my haste to make up for lost time."

"Charles Werthen, President."

"Present"

"Gladys Hardwood, Vice President."

"Present."

"Eleanor Werthen, Secretary"

"Present."

"Martha Olso, Treasurer."

"Here"

"Mary Lou Doceal, Member-at-large."

(Long pause) "Were you speaking to me?"

"Yes, Mary Lou, are you present?" asked Eleanor.

"Oh, yes I am present, quite present," smiled Marylou nodding her head affirmatively and putting down her knitting for the moment.

"Mr. Toddle, Executive Director."

"Yes?"

"Are you present or are you not?" Eleanor tapped her pencil in frustration.

Mr. Toddle, looking up from his notes, replied, "Of course, I am here. You asked me to attend."

"For the record, I will take that as a 'yes.' Mr. President, we have a quorum," announced Eleanor triumphantly.

Gladys ripped off her dark glasses and shot forth like a cobra striking when the flute stops. "As a resident of Toddle Manor for 18 years, I wish to know why you ever admitted that couple from California AND when you are going to get rid of them. The sooner, the better! Why did they leave California and come all the way here to Toddle Manor? Did you ask them that? Something is fishy about these two. They do not fit in!"

Mr. Toddle searched his meeting notes for a moment. Finding no such a category, he looked up at the five stern faces. All ten eyes, even the ones that only had 20/200 vision, bore down on him. "I beg your pardon, are you referring to Mr. and Mrs. Tanaka? Do I sense disharmony here? That is against our policy. May I refer you to the Manor Policy Manual? Indeed, I can give you the page - just a moment and I will check the index – disharmony ..."

"*They,* not we, are creating the disharmony. Tell *them* about page whatever! They have to go and soon!" countered Gladys.

Mr. Toddle struggled. The truth was that the Manor needed an infusion of cash and the Tanakas had it. Times had been hard. The market down, houses were not selling, and therefore move-ins were few. Occupancy was the lowest in decades. The Tanaka's were a wealthy prize. Toddle did not ask for specifics as to why they wanted to retire in the east; it was enough that they did! Toddle also sensed that the Tanakas might be looking for a good cause to support. That would reflect well on Toddle Manor either directly or indirectly. He knew some cultural issues would arise with a few of the residents. He rationalized that in a very short time acceptance would replace the ruffled feathers, that the Tanakas would adjust and that harmony would be restored. In measured tone and partial legal speak, Mr. Toddle explained, "May I remind you that Toddle Manor is a non-discriminatory organization that operates under the federal Americans with Disabilities Act? Any person who wishes to live here, has sufficient sustaining funds, passes the mental evaluation, does not have a chronic communicable disease and is able to care for him or herself independently is eligible for admission. A resident, for any reason, may elect to leave. How-ever, for the corporation to initiate such a move requires documentation of problems, conferences related to these issues, suggested remedies and subsequent non-compliance after three warnings. That is difficult if the resident in question is comfortable being here and is not disposed to relocation."

"Is there not an endangerment clause that could be employed?" asked Charles Werthen, proud of himself for remembering that word from his days on the admissions committee at Westchester University.

"If a resident is a danger to him or herself, or to other residents or staff, then yes, that resident may be relocated to an environment better equipped to handle the risk. Only one instance is required, if serious enough, such as serious abuse of self or others. I might note that this process is handled with the upmost confidentiality."

"Would loud noise be a reason?" asked Eleanor. As secretary of the Council, she was not taking notes having elected not to include any of this discussion in the minutes.

"Mrs. Werthen, loud is relative. How loud is too loud? If your sleep is disturbed on a regular basis, and repeated requests by the administration are ignored, then probably, yes," responded Mr. Toddle.

Martha spoke up, "Mr. Toddle, you have spoken of the need for diversity of residents in retirement communities for stimulating intellectual and cultural interactions. Does the admission of this new couple represent your attempt to initiate that notion here? I can tell you that there are *quite* a number of residents who are upset with a capital U. They flaunt our dress code, rock and roll music blares out over the south lawn from the open windows and they are naturists! Are you aware that they are naturists?"

"Naturists? Ah, no. Are they exposing themselves in common areas or just in the confines of their apartment?"

"Only in their apartment so far, but who knows what they have in mind! She talks of walks in the woods communing with nature. Who knows?"

Mr. Toddle, becoming slightly flushed at this topic, responded clinically. "We had one occasion about ten years ago when a resident used to walk naked deep in the woods beyond the south lawn. He was on our property, was fully dressed on entering and exiting the woods and went in an area that was not then and is not now used by the residents or staff for any purpose. It was only through the reporting of a chance sighting by a non-resident hiker, trespassing on the far boundary of the Manor grounds, that I found out. No resident was aware of the issue. It turned out that he had been doing this 'for his health' for eight years in good weather and was only discovered by a trick of fate. I investigated the statutes and local laws; he was not breaking any laws. What the Tanaka's do privately is not reproachable unless they expose themselves to other residents, staff or visitors.

"As for diversity, my goal is only to open the discussion for retirement communities as has occurred in the public schools where differing cultures have added to the enrichment of all."

"My culture is quite rich enough, thank you. We are retired and are supposed to be let alone to deteriorate peacefully at our own pace, not to be aggravated by a couple of hippies!" shot back Gladys.

Mr. Werthen asked, "Mr. Toddle, are you saying that you have no intention of removing these disturbing residents?"

"A defined breech of the rules as mentioned and the refusal to remedy such actions on three occasions would be necessary before such action could be contemplated. I will speak to them about the loud music, remind them to read the dress code and advise them on the rules related to nudity. Is there anything else you wish to discuss today?" Mr. Toddle asked looking at his watch as he started to rise.

"Speaking for all of us, we are not pleased and

will be looking for prompt results, Mr. Toddle, regarding the blaring music, violations of the dress code and the nudity. We will be watching for episodes of so called 'bad behavior.' Meeting adjourned," pronounced Charles tersely.

Gladys, Martha and Mary Lou were first to open the door of the conference room. Mary Lou screamed.

Gladys hollered, "What was that?"

Martha shouted, "Help!"

Gladys turned wide-eyed to Mr. Toddle, "I cannot believe my eyes. It looked like a

half-naked devil on wheels streaming fire and blood from head to knees!"

Mr. Toddle pushed through the doorway and looked up and down the hallway. It was empty. "Do you have any idea who it was, ladies?"

"It looked like a man with a bloody bandage on his head in an examining room gown on an electric cart, but I don't know who it was. He was going very fast, much too fast," Martha offered catching her breath.

"Well, I will call the security guard to look into this. I am terribly sorry that you were exposed

to such a shock. Please accept my apology.
Rest assured, I will find the perpetrator's
identity and deal with the situation. It should
not happen again," promised Mr. Toddle.

As everyone dispersed, Eleanor leaned toward
Charles and whispered, "Wait until dinner this
evening. This story will spread like wildfire!"
Charles smiled at Eleanor knowingly nodding his
head in agreement.

"Mr. Tanaka, please have a seat," smiled Mr. Toddle. "I have asked you to come in to discuss briefly one or two points regarding our community and group living in general. Sometimes new residents, who have been accustomed to living in their own homes, do not realize how particular activities might be a bit bothersome to their neighbors in this group living environment."

"Glad ya' brought it up, Bert. I'm glad ya' got it. This place is so grey, so sad. Life here is sooo generation. Shanti and me, we live big, open, free! I got big changes planned that will breathe life into this tired old beast! Get this, 'New Life Suites and Spa.'" Uki produced a small 3D color model of the new structure and placed it on Toddle's desk. "We build out next to the back wall. Three stories, horseshoe shape opening onto the south lawn – two story central gathering space, glass elevators to the 2nd and 3rd floor suites. Glass walls fer the first floor with computerized varying mood pastel coloring, two indoor/outdoor pools and hot tubs, one fer general use, one fer the naturists. Luxury suites, California open style. We leave the Manor as is – fer the ol' school set. Indoor and outdoor lounging areas, cascading fountain, tennis courts, bocce, hiking, biking trails, possibly horseback riding - open up the stables again." Uki's eyes glowed with the vision just like the good old days selling houses on the San Andreas Fault to Midwesterners. He could feel the rhythm coming back, and it felt good like smoking Oregon quality pot. "Sound stage, clear tiled dance floor with pressure activated pastel lighting different under each panel, seasonally colored lights in the palm trees. Bert, are you all right? You look strange."

Uki ran around the desk, catching Mr. Toddle just before he slid off his chair. He looked and felt like refrigerated cream cheese. "Easy Bert, put your head down between your knees, take a deep breath." Uki trickled cold water from the window sill thermos onto the back of his neck. "Atta boy, atta boy, shake it off. OK, Bert. Can you hear me, Bert?"

Mr. Toddle leaned back, "I'm wet. Do we have a water pipe break? What happened?" His eyes focused. "Oh, you! Oh, I remember-- some crazy idea. Oh, no." Coming to full alert, "Mr. Tanaka, have you gone mad? Toddle Manor was, is now and always will be a distinguished life care community for discerning residents. It will not be turned into some wild place. Period! And that is final! Period!"

"You are going bankrupt, Bert. Think ahead. How does the future look?"

Mr. Toddle leaned forward, "What did you say?" Then in hushed tones, "Where did you hear that?"

"In each of the last 8 quarters, Toddle Manor has lost money. You're sinking, Bert. Break even occupancy here is 80%. Two years ago, occupancy was 75%, last year, 73%, this year's projection is 70%. Now I can help..."

"How did you get these data? These figures are confidential and completely secured! You have been hacking into our financial program. I will have you arrested!"

"Stay cool, Bert. Take three deep breaths. Catch this. I can float this boat. All ya' have ta' do is relax and let it happen. Be cool. Get this picture: A bistro, indoor and outdoor dining, lounge chairs with stereo speakers in the head rests, arm rest extension for mini television, voice selection or finger-tip channel selectors. Sweeping contoured roof extending out over the new expanded patio. Circular drive extension to a grand entrance for the new wing. We're talking 85% occupancy before breaking ground and a projected 100% at completion. The New Life Center offers classes for healthy cooking, meditation, Tai Chi, yoga, circle chanting, nature walking – future residents invited. Give the public what they want, and they'll stand in line to buy. Trust me," Uki zoned in. "Soak it in. Suites selling for 50% over your current rates, a full house, 20% net revenue over expenses. You will save this lovely, classic, family home that you and your family have worked so hard to preserve. I always say, progress is coming like a bus; get on board first and steer."

Mr. Toddle rose to his full height of 5 feet 7 inches, eyes blazing, "Mr. Tanaka, if you think you can come in here …"

Uki stood, magically producing a color, handsomely retouched photo of Mr. Toddle with a headline, "CCRC Business Journal's Man of the Year, Norbert Adams Toddle III. Melding the modern with the traditional, Toddle has created a brilliant concept community outside of Philadelphia. Cover story, page one."

"What is this? Where did it come from? How did you get it? Let me see that." Toddle reaches across the desk, studies the cover page and thumbs through the magazine. Looking up, "This is last month's issue with a fake cover. You did this!"

"How does it feel to be man of the year, Bert? That can be you and soon. My grand plan would do that for ya' - oh yeah. Famous. Top speaking fees, travel with your wife. Many more articles about your success. Make Toddle Manor a financial success for the future. I'll leave the magazine and the 3D model with you. You need some quiet time." Toddle stood looking quizzically at the cover unaware of Uki's departure.

CHAPTER 9   THE FOOD COMMITTEE

Shanti opened the clubroom door, "Cool, a
good group here already! I'm Shanti. Glad you
all came this morning to talk about vegetarian
and organic foods. Let's be a vegetarian food
committee together. I feel powerful chi here.
We'll make up dinner menus and meet regularly
with Jeff Stuffsom. So, let's form a circle, and
I'll hand out a list of wholesome organic
vegetarian foods to start with. We can add on
to it as we warm up." Looking around,
"Awesome, there are six of us here – that
should be a good working group. We can mark
down the days of the week next to foods we
pick and hand them in at the end. Who wants
to start? Say your first name and your choices.
Yes," nodding to the trim grey-haired woman
with glasses on her right.

"I've been here 12 years, and everyone knows
my name. It's Charlene Gardenier. I am a
retired registered dietitian, and I am relieved
that finally we will get some attention to
healthy eating. We have always had sufficient
food for the non-gluttonous majority, but red
meat with brown gravy, mashed potatoes with
brown gravy and overcooked vegetables is
hardly healthy fare. My choice for Sunday's
main meal would be salmon with parsley and
lemon, kale, and sweet potato. For a salad:
avocado, tomato, finely ground almonds and

fresh blueberries with a light vinaigrette dressing. For dessert: fresh fruit and assorted low fat, low cholesterol cheeses. A list of the calories, saturated fat and carbohydrate content of each selection should be available for all entrees daily."

"Supreme, Charlene. Sounds wonderful. Good idea about a fact sheet. Who's next?"

The overweight grey-haired woman with glasses next to Charlene spoke up. "I am Stout, Greta Stout. I love to eat. I hate soy. I hate exercising. I have come here today to learn how to lose weight. If I eat vegetarian foods will they taste as good as regular? Will I lose thirty pounds long enough to get into my grandmother of the bride's dress again? I have a wedding coming up in three months."

Over the muffled side comments, Shanti said, "Most of the foods on the list are ones you are used to. They'll be cooked and seasoned differently and will be less fattening. Quantity still must be controlled. Calories are calories all the same. Once you decide to do this and achieve your goal then stay with it. You will feel sooo much better. Greta, we will all be wishing you well and cheering you on. We are a lovin' group and excited about your weight loss plan. We will help every way you want us to."

"Thank you."

"Ola, across over there, what is it you want to say? "

"I am Clara Renderly," volunteered a medium sized woman with grey hair and glasses. "Why don't we have more shell fish, like shrimp? That was my husband's favorite Saturday night dinner when he was alive."

"Yes, they are nutritious."

A knock at the clubroom door; everyone turned. Shanti rose and moved toward the door, "That must be Jeff Stuffsom. I asked him to join us." Opening the door Shanti smiled very warmly and cooed, "Jeff, thank ya' sooo much for your interest in upgrading the menu of Toddle Manor. Welcome and join our first meeting of the Vegetarian Food Committee. I'm sure you know all these fine gals. Have a seat here, next to me."

Jeff was a bit taken aback. He thought the group wanted to have the usual gripe session that he has had to weather from time to time. "Ah hello, thank you for the invitation. Can you tell me what you are discussing?"

"We want healthier food. Vegetarian food," they all shouted almost in unison. Surprising themselves and definitely surprising Jeff, who reflexively jolted back in his chair as the shock wave hit him.

"Well, ah well, I ah mean, we have never had a specific vegetarian menu, but we do offer vegetables to choose from at dinner each evening."

"Peas and succotash that have had the nutrition steamed out of them are hardly nutritious choices," interrupted Charlene. "We 're talking about fresh, al dente, rich, vibrant-looking green vegetables; green beans, broccoli, kale, spinach. What's the problem?"

Greta chimed in, "Yes, why tough overcooked flat iron steak or dry roast beef and why brown gray with every entree? And another thing, what is in the Friday evening mystery balls? They taste like sawdust! The chicken breasts are dry, tough and stringy. Why not baked and stuffed with spinach or mushrooms with a light ginger sauce? And your cherry pie is made with canned cherries, really!"

A chorus of "yes, yes" followed.

Jeff Stuffsom stood up and backed toward the door, "I don't control the finances of the culinary department. I have a budget. I would have to meet with my chefs, do a cost assessment and then meet with Mr. Toddle. This might not be the best time to request increased kitchen staff and food allowance. Let me get back to you in a month or two." As he bolted for the door he heard, "That's too long. Make it two weeks!"

The room erupted in whoops and laughter releasing their suppressed long-suffering from bland and boring meals. Just how many Wednesdays of creamed chipped beef on toast can one tolerate in silence?

After the meeting broke up, Shanti invited everyone interested to come and join her forest walking group that was gathering on the south lawn for a naturist walk.

Among those in the group was Mary Lou, who had been told by Gladys to wave if and when the group was going to disrobe. Gladys and Martha were going to stealthy maneuver up close enough to take pictures of Shanti in the nude.

When the group set off rhythmically swaying their arms and humming. Mary Lou brought up the rear and turned to be sure she saw Gladys and Martha moving down the lawn in the same general direction. Deeper into the woods the naturists went, and in a small clearing Shanti quickly shed her muumuu, her only garment, with a sigh of freedom, a stretch and a laugh of joy. The others followed her lead.

By chance, Uki happened to be weeding his Marijuana patch nearby. He could not see the women and men, but he could hear some distant laughter. Shanti had never been to his little garden and was unaware that she had ventured close to it. Then in a break in the foliage Uki glimpsed Mary Lou about 50 yards away hurrying down a narrow path waving her arms. Within minutes, Mary Lou hurried back. What was this? Uki slid into the brush and waited. Within minutes, breaking branches, ouches and grunts signaled Gladys and Martha's arrival on the path. They moved stealthily forward. Uki followed at a distance.

"There she is! Wish I looked like that," mused Martha.

Gladys, pulling the brambles out of her short scraggly brunette hair, whispered, "Shush, let me get my camera out. I can take some good pictures from here, but I don't want to get Mary Lou in them."

While Gladys took pictures of Shanti, Uki positioned himself for good profile shots of Gladys and Martha with out-of-focus naturists in the background. When he was satisfied with quality and quantity, Uki labeled them "peeping Thomasettas" and e-mailed them off to Charles Werthen with the question, "What disciplinary action will the Residents' Council take against these residents, or should these photos go to Bert?" He thought, *hopefully, this will defang any beginning conspiracy.*

CHAPTER 10   FIRE!

After dinner, Uki was toking his favorite weed in his trailer when a fire started behind him. Engrossed in working with 3-D printing of the New Life plans, he did not notice that the ash he had flicked into the waste basket was not entirely cold. The smoldering ember was enough to ignite crumpled failed paper trials. Thinking that that was a sign to take a break, Uki sat back to enjoy smoking and gazing into the fire.

 The CZX7000's shrill alarm screamed, "FIRE! FIRE! Evacuate immediately! Calling 911. FIRE! FIRE! Evacuate immediately! Calling 911. FIRE, FI...." Uki slowly woke up and hit the stop alarm button. Smoke filled the forward half of the trailer. As he bolted toward the rear door, the siren got louder and louder. It crossed Uki's mind that his phone did not have a siren alarm. As he turned the rear door handle, the door suddenly jerked open ejecting him out of the trailer. Firemen pushed past him, "Turn it on, Al. Full on."

"Oh, no! Don't do it! I have valuable drawings and electronics in there," shouted Uki. The sound of high-pressure water hurling desks, printers, chairs, tables and plans against the forward wall drown out his pleas. Axes tore through the side walls and roof, water spewing out with very blow.

"Ok Al shut down the pump. The chief looked at his stop watch, "Ten minutes. That's good. Clean up, men. Let's get back to the fire house. "You own this trailer?" Chief Martin Waller asked pulling his clipboard from the fire truck's glove box and a pen from under his yellow slicker.

Uki looked up from the curb where he was sitting with his head in his hands. The blackened, smoking, smoldering, and sagging wreck drained water from every crevice. "What trailer?" Uki moaned.

"Look mister, we saved your life and put out the fire. Looks like it started in a plastic waste basket. Hope you got insurance. What's your name? I gotta file a report."

Uki rallied. "Uki Tanaka."

"You live here?"

"Yeah."

"Print your name and Sign in three places."

"I wanna read it, first."

"It says that your life and your property were saved and that the fire department is not responsible for any damage that may have been necessary to extinguish the fire. You can sign it here or take your time reading it carefully down at the firehouse where there is good light."

"Pen? "

"Here, sign in three places."

Uki signed and returned the form and pen.

"Did I hear a 'Thank you', Sir? We are all volunteers, you know. I was watching the ball game with my kids when this call came in. I dropped everything and raced to your assistance...."

"Yeah, you're cool." Uki went around to the front of the trailer where there was little damage, unlocked and opened a lower exterior compartment. He stepped back when water cascaded down over his sandals. When the flow stopped, he reached in and pulled out 4 wet brown plastic bags that clinked together despite careful handling. He gave one of these to each of the firemen. "Chief, thanks. Here is my tax-deductible contribution to your health and welfare fund."

"That's thoughtfully phrased and gratefully

received. We will deposit them as soon as possible. Sid, you got to the firehouse second so you get to drive home. Start 'er up. Climb on, men and let's go."

"Marty, the fire hose! "

"Stop! Buck, get down and reel in the damn hose. Where is your head? Don't tell me."

With a parting blast of the air horn and two whoops of the siren, the brave men of Hook and Ladder Company #1 disappeared over the summit of the drive to the waves of residents who had packed the roof garden railing atop The Gardens assisted living facility adjacent to Adams and Lincoln wings. Such excitement!

Uki sifted through the soaked debris for the sketches and the plans that he had just completed. They were ruined but legible enough to be helpful for a reproduction. The computer and 3-D printer had been totaled. Uki touched the CZX7000 search mode. "The nearest large trailer sales center."

"Reminder. This will be a duplicate purchase," responded his CZX7000.

"'Toad One' just burned - totally," responded Uki.

"Ah, how did that happen?"

"I said, where is the near..."

"All right, all right. 1335 US Route 202 North. I cannot pronounce the company name; Pennsylvania German. See spelling."

"Rating?"

"5 star. 200 trailers on the lot."

"Log name and address into GPS," ordered Uki.

"We are sorry to hear of the demise of 'Toad One'," noted CZX7000, "Shall I notify insurance now or do you need time to make it look like an accident?"

Uki shut off search mode muttering, "Smart ass," turning it off then on again. "Search on-line for 3-D printers. Show me the upgrade models from Panamerican-Paneuropean-Panpacific Electronics, Inc."

***

Well after dark that evening, Olive Tipplemore had settled down in her soft bed in The Gardens assisted living. For eight years, she had lived in Jefferson wing and loved it there, but she started needing some extra help with activities of daily living. The Gardens was the right place for her now. Two months had passed since the move to assisted living, she was becoming accustomed to the surroundings and was quite comfortable and satisfied. As she often did when drifting off to sleep, she started dreaming of being in her old apartment. She suddenly awoke. "Smoke! I smell smoke! Help! Call 911!" Olive picked up the bedside phone and dialed 911. "Hello, hello. Help. Fire! "

"Where are you mam? What's your name?"

"I'm at Toddle Manor. The 2nd floor of the Jefferson wing. Number, ah, ah, number J222. Hurry! Olive Tipplemore. Hurry! I have to run to the fire escape. Goodbye." Olive ran out into the hall. Glendora Hepless had opened the window and was turning on the microwave fan. "Whooee! We had some real smoke from that cinnamon roll! So small but so burned up! I should have warmed it 10 seconds, not 30 seconds. Woof!" Turning around CNA Hepless said, "Ms. Tipplemore could you smell the smoke in your room?"

Reorienting, Olive replied, "Yes, it woke me up. I thought there was a fire. I was going to the fire escape."

"Well don't worry. Everything is under control. Would you like a cup of tea?"

"No thank you, I'll be all right. I can go right back to sleep."

"Well good night then – sorry I disturbed you. I'll be more careful this time, and Mr. Courterman will just have to wait a little longer for his cinnamon roll."

"Good night." Olive returned to her room, snuggled down in her soft comfortable bed again and drifted off into a mystical other world.

"Watch how y'er drivin', Buck," slurred Chief Waller over the wail of the siren as he

hung on around the sharp turn into the Toddle Manor drive.

Buck hiccoughed, "Where to?"

"Around the courtyard to the other side and stop." Skidding to an abrupt stop, Al was jerked free of his hold on the chrome siderail and came up under a large azalea bush.

"Axes, men. Al, while you're down there, get the hose out and be ready to go up through a window. OK, Ready?"

Three axe men headed for the veranda door. Forcing it open with brute force they ran up the stairs to the second floor of Jefferson. Funny –

no smoke or flames. No fire alarm going off.
222 – no name on the door. The Chief pounded
on the door. "Fire Department, open up, open
up. Fire Department."   No answer, no sounds
inside. "She must be overcome with smoke.
Break it down, men." This original solid ash
door proved sturdier than the veranda door.
"Axes, hurry!"

Bell Darple was exhausted from the moving-in
process. Forty years in the same house in West
Chester and the winnowing out to move into a
one-bedroom apartment had been stressful.
But by nightfall the essentials had been
unpacked and in their proper places. She felt
good about the day and went to bed early. In
addition to the routine removal of her glasses,
hearing aids, and use of an eye shield, she put
in ear plugs and took a sleeping pill to
guarantee a good solid night's sleep.

She was jolted out of her sleep by being shaken
by the shoulders. "Are you all right? Wake up!
Where's the fire," shouted Chief Waller while
the other 2 tripped through the center of the
splintered door. Buck hiccoughed again, and
Sol giggled pointing at Buck. "Break down every
door and look for flames," ordered the Waller.

Bell opened her eyes and saw blackness.
Thrashing about and screaming, "Help, help,"
she managed to get the eye shield off one eye
and untangle her legs from the bed clothes.
Standing up she saw the blurred image of a

large yellow creature with waving arms and moving mouth. She heard no sound except her own screams, "Help, Yellow Invaders, help me, call the police!" Breaking free she ran into the hall screaming and was stopped by George Jackson, the security guard. He had run to Jefferson 2 when he heard the fire truck siren and the crashing about of the firemen.

"Hold on, Ms. Darple, hold on. What happened?" The guard looked up and said, "Hi Marty, what going on? Is there a fire? Our alarm and sprinklers did not activate."

"Hi George, we got a 911 fire called in from an Olive Tipplemore in apartment J222 but we ain't findin' no fire. We're gonna have ta' call the police to handle this," said the Chief.

"This is Ms. Bell Darple. She just moved into that apartment today which, I might add, has just been completely renovated for her. Ms. Olive Tipplemore moved out two months ago. She is in The Gardens assisted living. Ms. Darple, did you call the fire department?"

Bell, now awake and, at a distance of six inches, could recognize his face and uniform, looked up at him and said," What? Speak up. I don't have my hearing aids in."

"Did you call the fire department," George yelled in her ear.

"No. Did you?" George pulled up a chair and seated Bell. "I'll call The Gardens on the walkie talkie. Security to The Gardens, come back." Static. "The Gardens, nurse Hepless speaking."

"Did you or Ms. Tipplemore call the fire department?"

Long pause. "I burned a cinnamon bun in the microwave, and the smell of smoke woke up Ms. Tipplemore. But it did not set off the alarm. I opened the window and turned on the fan. We were fine, and she went back to bed; so, no, we did not have a fire. "

"Did she call 911 before she came out and saw you?" asked George.

"I didn't ask her. I don't think so. She came right out and was heading for the fire escape when we saw each other."

"Please ask her that question for me. The Fire department is here with me on J2nd floor and we need to confirm who called them out," said the guard.

"Oh, I hate to wake her again, but if it's that important, just a minute." There were shuffling steps, a door latch clicks and then a soft voice, "Ms. Tipplemore..., Ms. Tipplemore..., It's Glendora, your nurse. Ms. Tipplemore wake up

80

I need to ask you a question."

"What? What is it?"

"When you smelled smoke from the cinnamon bun burning did you call 911?"

A pause while Olive got her thoughts together. "Yes, I did, but then you told me there was no fire so everything was all right, and I don't blame you. That could have happened to anyone."

"Did you call 911 back to tell them it was a false alarm?"

"No dear, they would not come if there was no fire. Good night and don't worry about it another minute, Glendora, you're sweet." Olive rolled over and pulled the cover up over her head.

CHAPTER 11   THE BUS TRIP TO THE SHORE

It was a beautiful day for the trip. Rhonda's prayer for good weather had been answered. As the residents filed out onto the front drive, assisted by Rhonda and Wanda Thump, the Toddle Manor bus pulled up, stopped with a squeak of brakes, and Hal stepped out of the driver's door. "Good morning everyone. Lovely day. Are you ready for a trip to Atlantic City?"

"You think this old clunker will make it to Atlantic City and back?" asked Earl.

"Just because this ol' Bluebird has a hard ride, doesn't mean it's ready for the junk yard. They built these buses well. How-ever, I will admit that the springs and shocks feel like they were made for trucks not passenger vehicles so we do get some bumpiness on the road."

"Bumpiness! I'd 'a been thrown outta my seat if it weren't for the seat belt! Well, stay away from the potholes; they'll break your teeth or your back."

"Let's get aboard now. We'll give a hand up, if you need it. We will have a full bus so do move to the back and choose a seat as soon as possible. Wanda Thump, will help you board while I stow the walkers. Thank you." After Hal locked the storage area, he scanned the courtyard for stragglers. Seeing none he climbed on board and produced a clip board. Using the microphone, he addressed the riders, "Please put a check in front of your name as I pass this roster down the aisle so I know that everyone that signed up is here." Hal checked the gauges as he started the engine; all swung into the normal range. The clip board roster was returned. "Everyone except Isabel Larken was checked off. Has anyone seen Ms. Larken?"

"She is always late, Hal," several passengers called out. Here she comes, now." Big applause broke out as Isabel is helped aboard and buckled into her seat.

"Rather confused by all the clapping, Isabel asked her seat mate, "It looks like we are all here 30 minutes early. By the way, where are we going shopping today?"

"Atlantic City."

"Oh, really. Is this a sale day?"

"Most of the folks are going to play the slot machines and have lunch."

"Tell me about these slot machines. Is that gambling?"

"The machine has coins inside. You put coins into it and pull the level. If you are lucky you get more money back than you put in - you win. If you don't get anything back, then you lose."

"We are ready to depart. Be sure your seat belts are fastened. Raise your hand if you are having a problem. We all need to be secure before starting off." No difficulties were noted and with a lurch and a cloud of exhaust the Toddle Bluebird turned and went down the drive then east on Route 1 N to the waves and cheers of Rhonda and Wanda Thump.

CHAPTER 12   THE CONVENTION

Norbert Adams Toddle III's hands perspired as he reviewed his power point presentation and notes. *Even great warriors perspire before battle. It's OK,* he reasoned. However, there was a persistent little voice in his ear, "This is your opportunity for national exposure, Norbert, to be equally or even better known for humanitarian service than your state senator grandfather. Do not fall short*!*"

The doorbell chimed.

 "I 'll get it," Drusilla called up the stairs as she crossed the foyer. Opening the front door, she saw a uniformed chauffeur. Looking beyond him, she thrilled at the midnight blue Rolls Royce stretch limousine.

"Good morning, Mrs. Toddle. My name is Claude. I am here to drive Mr. Toddle to Convention Hall for his keynote address and panel discussion. Following the presentation, I will return Mr. Toddle here. At 5:30 P.M. I will return to escort you both to The Union League for the reception and dinner. Do you have any questions or special requests?" Recapturing her composure, Drusilla smiled, "You seem to have everything nicely under control. I will let Mr. Toddle know that you are here."

"That being the case, I will wait in the limo. Thank you, Ma'am." Claude touched his cap brim with two gloved fingers, turned and strode to the Rolls not looking to right or left.

As Drusilla closed the door, she was quite sure Claude must have spent significant time in the military. Drusilla's father had been career Army, and she knew that carriage and stride whenever she saw it. Walking to the stairs, she called up, "That was, Claude, your chauffeur. He is waiting for you in the limousine."

"Chauffeur? Limousine? Really?" Norbert came down in his best navy-blue business suit (his burial suit) and brief case in hand. Smiling at Drusilla, "I should be back by midafternoon. If anyone calls, take a message, and I will call back."

"Yes, dear. Good luck and enjoy yourself." Drusilla gave him a reassuring smile and a wisp of a kiss on the cheek.

As Norbert walked down the front steps, he suddenly snapped out of his anxiety to behold the limousine.

"Good morning Mr. Toddle. My name is Claude," he said, opening the rear door of the Rolls. Norbert, still in awe over the fine machine, missed his step down the curb but recovered enough to semi-gracefully enter the rear leather seat. When the door closed, Norbert momentarily felt hermetically sealed in the rear compartment with tinted windows and a glass slide separating him from the driver. The limousine moved out silently down Meeting House Lane then up around the hill toward US Route 1.

Toddle picked up the phone in the arm rest. "Claude, can you hear me?" No response. Louder, "Can you hear me?" Again, no response. Finally, he shouted, "CAN YOU HEAR ME?" This time his thumb accidentally depressed the "push to talk" button on the phone handle.

The limousine jerked right, tires squealing. Claude stabilized the Rolls, righted his cap and himself and responded, "Yes Sir, I can hear you very clearly when you depress the 'push to talk' button on the hand grip. It is under your thumb if you are right handed. Speak in a normal tone if you do not mind. Thank you, Sir."

Norbert mentally went through his address much as a downhill ski racer envisions his run before entering the starting gate. They curled right from US 1 by-pass onto I-476 south.

"Is the Rolls Royce yours?" Norbert pushed to talk.

"No, sir. I drive it when requested by the Mr. Tanaka or Shanti."

"Why do you use the name, Shanti, instead of Mrs. Tanaka?"

"I was told that she only has one name, Shanti, not Mrs. anyone. Am I wrong about that, Sir?" Claude asked looking in the rearview mirror.

Now Toddle was confused. He thought what if they are not married? Living at Toddle Manor and not married - what a scandal! He pushed that thought into outer space. There was more than enough on his plate for today. Ah, a woman with independent wealth or a stage name or both. That's it. He could live with that.

"Are you on a retainer or paid by the assignment, if I may ask?"

"I can tell you that all our transactions for trips, elapsed time, fuel and maintenance are compensated for on the basis of units," answered Claude a bit reluctantly.

Norbert realized that he had over-stepped propriety. What is a unit? He decided it was better to drop the subject and review his opening remarks one more time. He reached forward, unlatched and extended the desk top and opened his case on it. I-95 slid silently by underneath the Rolls heading north towards the Convention Center.

"Thank you for coming to this off-site luncheon
meeting. Hopefully you will find the cuisine to
your liking. I am Mr. Tanaka. As I mentioned
over the telephone, I represent the Toddle
Manor real estate office. While you settle
yourselves and order beverages of choice and
meals from the menu, I would like to present a
power point of our property with the new
building and its setting. We will entertain your
questions and provide answers to your
satisfaction. To proceed with our plans, today
we need your tentative approval for expansion
by a show of hands. This first slide shows the
horseshoe shaped three story 'New Life Suites
and Spa' abutting the southern exposure of the
Manor. The patio is extended as a lounge area.
Note the two indoor-outdoor swimming pools.
There will be soft indirect lighting that dims
from 10 PM to 6AM. As you can see there is
one glass enclosed elevator with a view of the
south lawn in each wing of the horseshoe.
Earthen roof garden, solar panels and
geothermal heating combination are calculated
to make the project energy neutral and green in
keeping with the township's goal to be certified
as a 'Green Community.' The existing drive to
the stables parking area will be completed
around on the east side to make a full circle
back to the front courtyard as you see here.
There will be additional parking off this new

segment on the east side of the new construction as noted on this enlarged view. Regarding green space, given our extensive acreage, the expanded foot print is well within the ratio required by the township. No change of zoning will be necessary. That concludes my brief overview. I see your entrees are being served. Please enjoy the luncheon and fellowship. I will be happy to answer your questions.

"When you have finished dessert, please study the 3-D model on the table against the wall to your left. The exhibit shows the New Life area in pastel green; the Manor is in tan. Then before we conclude I would ask for your general approval of the project so that I may continue to plan, get estimates for construction and initiate permits for phase one."

"Mr. Tanaka, my name is Ted Johnson. I'm a lawyer. Was this Norbert Toddle's idea and has he approved the plan as presented?"

"Certainly. We have discussed this plan in detail, and he has seen a 3-D model. I can assure you that he was very excited at the presentation. Quite overcome."

"Why is he not here? This is a big project. Mr. Toddle is a very conservative person."

"He would have been here, but through a

scheduling error, he had to be at the Convention Center to present this concept in a Keynote address and to chair the follow-up panel before the American Organization of CCRCs. I understand he is well regarded nationally. He is seen as an executive who can bring into a community new wealth, new residents and new construction all of which stimulate the local community with jobs and patronage of local businesses. As you know senior citizens in CCRCs tend to be very responsible finance-ally, do not use the public schools and vote in a higher percentage than any other age group.

"Take this project, the New Life Suites and Spa, the cost will approximate $ 1.5 million initially, using all local workers and materials. All local business will benefit, and school tax revenue will increase without increased student enrollment – the ideal scenario. "Are there any other questions?" Uki asked, his face flushed with the surge of endorphins.

"Do you have the funding arranged? We do not want to have a project started but not completed," wondered Olin Swindell, a banker.

"There are several granting agencies that provide construction funds for innovative senior living pilot projects. It is highly likely that we will be completely funded. Also, the Manor is debt free, and if needed, a new mortgage would cover the project. Rest assured the new addition will be completed. Groundbreaking will begin when 75% of the units have been sold. Sales are anticipated to be brisk with virtually 100% of the units sold at the time the building is ready for occupancy. Are there any other questions? At your place setting is my business card. Call me at any time should there be points needing clarification. When you finished studying the model on the table, give me your comments and suggestions before we take the straw vote."

While the commissioners were engrossed in the model, Uki opened a large box from under the central dining table and had the waiter place a tall narrow blue and white gift-wrapped box at each place setting. For the next 30 minutes, Uki fielded questions until there were no more.

"Now that you have seen our project, how many here would be likely to approve the construction of this environmentally friendly, income producing, job creating, green and beautiful residence at the rear of Toddle Manor?"

As the hands went up, Uki noted with pride that he had not lost his touch although it had been stressful speaking in gram-matically correct eastern English. "Gentlemen, I thank you for your confidence, and we will be submitting formal plans as soon as possible. As you leave, please note there is a small favor at your place.

Again, thank you for your attendance and your cooperation. This concludes our meeting. Do have a good afternoon."

Uki shook hands at the door and smiled as he checked for favorable body language. He thought of Bert and hoped he was achieving a good response to his speech. Uki also hoped he could keep this meeting under wraps until the right time.

Having managed to pirate a copy of Toddle's speech 2 days before, Uki had already written several glowing reviews. They will be good supplements for the grants that were otherwise ready for submission.

He checked the time. Yes, he could run up to Harrisburg for the meeting with the medical marijuana lobbyist. Satisfied, he tipped each of the staff with a "unit," duly noting each in the ledger as he settled into the contoured seat of the Alfa Romeo. He buckled up, adjusted the mini-microphone and ear buds beneath his Harrisburg Senators baseball cap, and started the engine.

Meanwhile at Toddle Manor, Charles Werthen had gathered the band of five together for a hastily called meeting in the Werthen's apartment. When everyone was seated and Eleanor had served tea, Charles asked, "Gladys have you or Martha seen these photos?" He handed his lap top to them to share.

"Where did you get these," Gladys burst out. Martha's face turned crimson as she drew in a quick breath and shut her eyes hard

Mary Lou squealed, "Oh, pictures. Pictures of us together? Let me see too," as she got up and looked over Martha's shoulder. "Well, I guess I'm not in these, but they are good of you two, don't you think? That was the other day when you asked me to let you know where we were walking because you would have never ever found us other-wise."

"Oh, be quiet, Mary Lou," snorted Gladys.

Charles answered, "Uki Tanaka sent them to me. He asked what action the Residents Council would take against peeking Toms, or whether the photos should be sent to Mr. Toddle for further disciplinary action. This places all five of us in a difficult situation. It is one thing to be alert to activities by the Tanakas that could have them removed as residents, but it is quite another to set out purposely to spy on and to secretly photograph them or any other residents. Gladys and Martha and Mary Lou, you must promise not to engage in any further inciting behavior. Eleanor and I will not be part of any such activity nor will we support or protect you should you become involved again. As far as these photographs are concerned, I will tell Mr. Tanaka, truthfully, that the executive committee of the Residents Council met in a closed-door session with you ladies and that you were remorseful and would not interfere with the nature walks in the future. Is that agreeable?"

Martha nodded and said, "Yes, I should have never gotten involved in the first place."

"I grudgingly agree," Gladys muttered through her teeth.

"I was just trying to help my two friends. What is wrong with that? We are supposed to be friendly and helpful," complained Mary Lou.

"We have to be considerate of everyone, not just two friends, but I doubt that you will be drawn into any further schemes. I hope Uki will accept our response as sufficient justice and that the issue will be closed," said Charles. "Thank you for coming on such short notice."

CHAPTER 14   UKI SAVES THE DAY

Driving back from Harrisburg, Uki was light-hearted. The meeting was productive, and the lobbying was going well. The luncheon meeting with the township commissioners had gone well, so this had been a very good day. Uki again wondered how Toddle's presentation had been received and, checking the dash board clock, he noticed it was about time for Clyde to be driving the Toddles to the reception. Clyde was totally dependable. Everything was under control. Strangely Uki was uneasy. Things were going too well – often a bad sign for Uki. He checked the gas gauge, oil pressure, rpm's, tire pressure and engine temperature for potential trouble – all in normal range. Nevertheless, Uke decided that he would check at the desk for problems when he arrived back at the Manor. He was only 10 minutes away.

This uneasy feeling was strong enough that Uki drove to the front door instead of parking behind the barn and walking up the south lawn. He found Rhonda on two phone lines and clearly distressed. "What's cookin', love child?" Seeing Uki Rhonda hung up both phones.

"Mr. Tanaka, please, this is serious. Hal, our bus driver, called in. He was coming back from Atlantic City with the residents when he hit a pothole and apparently the front axle broke.

Hal is going with the tow truck to assess to damage. The residents were shaken up a bit, but no one was injured. They are in Jack's Truck Stop at the Newport exit of route 141 in Delaware south of Wilmington. We have a second bus but it is in the shop for an inspection and that driver is off duty. Security does not have a vehicle large enough to carry 24 residents, Mr. Toddle is out for the day at a convention, and I am afraid to disturb him. I left a voice message for Mr. Werthen, but he has not called back after 20 minutes. Frankly, I don't know what anyone other than Mr. Toddle could do."

"How many residents down there, Love?"

"Twenty-four and it's getting late. They are going to miss dinner. I'll have to ask culinary to pack cold lunches for them when they get here."

"I gotcha covered, girl. Kick back and be cool, I'll bring 'em home safe, fed and happy."

Uki exited by the front door, buckled himself into the Alfa Romeo. He powered up his CZX7000, "Connect me to a charter bus service in Wilmington, Delaware and ring back when you have the manager." Uki switched on the GPS, "Program the fastest route this time of day from here to Jack's Truck Stop, Newport exit, route 141, Delaware"

"CZX7000 connection ready. Mr. Condolloza on line."

"Mr. Condolloza, this is Uki Tanaka. I am in charge of transportation, tourism and marketing for a large senior's corporation in Pennsylvania, and I need an urgent service from you. Obviously if this is well per-formed and executed, you will receive considerable future business from us." Uki explained the situation emphasizing the shaken, distraught and frail nature of these aged residents. Mr. Condolloza responded to this call to arms and promised to immediately dispatch a top of the line air ride diesel coach with lavatory, WIFI and a television at each seat. "These poor people will miss dinner at the Manor. Will you please contact your concierge service for a ground hostess to serve dinner on board: steak, duchess potatoes, mixed vegetables, garden salad and chocolate and blonde brownies. To drink, four magnums of champagne and two dozen flutes. I am sure you can handle that. Let me give you a credit card number. Your prompt and courteous service is greatly appreciated. Please add a 30% gratuity to this entire order of coach, driver, hostess, food and services. I will meet the coach personally at Jack's Truck Stop. Call me back at this number if there are any problems or delays. In your capable hands, I certainly do not expect any. Thank you and good-bye."

Reprogrammed, the Alfa Romeo enjoyed the full throttle run, purring south towards Jack's. Uki called Shanti telling her why he would be late for dinner and asked her to save a take-out vegi plate for him. He relaxed in the seat, streaming rock and roll through his ear buds, and smiled. It *is* cool to have money.

Two hours later the gleaming purple and yellow air ride tour bus was loaded with happy and excited residents after the attractive smiling hostess served Champagne and then the steaming hot entrees from the catering truck alongside. The uniformed driver checked seat belts and asked if everyone was ready to go. Waving their flutes in a salute of affirmation, the residents called out, "Let's go!" The bus curled out north onto route 141 heading for home. Uki smiled and waved good-bye amidst a rousing cheer of "Uki saved the day." Getting into his roadster, he noticed an older woman coming out of Jack's and desperately looking about. He drove over to her, "May I help ya', Mam?"

"Oh, I think I missed the bus back to Toddle Manor. Did they leave without me? What will I do?"

"I'm goin' to Toddle Manor right now. I'm Uki Tanaka. I live there too. Bet you're Isabel Larken, aren't ya'?"

"Yes, but how did you know that?"

"Some residents on the bus mentioned that an

Isabel Larken was always late for trips, so I thought..."

"I am never late! For some reason, our buses always leave a half-hour early!"

"Hop in and I'll drive ya' home. You missed dinner on the bus, but I was given a complimentary bottle of champagne if you would like some of that. We could grab a sandwich from Jack's before we leave."

"I can't eat riding in a car. I get sick, but yes, thank you, to Champagne. I should celebrate even though I missed the bus. You know I won $17,000 from that slot machine today. That will be enough champagne; this *is* a water tumbler. Don't drive too fast; I don't want to spill any. Nice car. My daddy had an open Ford when I was very young. I sat in the rumble seat. Do you remember rumble seats? I used to climb in on a step in the rear fender. A little more Champagne if you please. It's quite good. This is fun. My hair is short now so it doesn't matter if it blows around. Mine is shorter than yours. Why do you wear long hair? Winters don't get that cold any more. It's some sort of a hippy thing, I guess. Well, when I was young we had really cold snowy winters. Why don't you hand me that Champagne bottle? I'd like you to keep both hands on the wheel. It seems like we are going faster. Are you speeding up? I don't care if I miss dinner, ha, ha, so don't hurry on my account. Do you know how to get back to

Tudder Minnel? I hope so because I have no idea where we are, tee hee hee. I bet you could be quite an interesting man if you shaved and stopped wearing gaudy shirts and shorts, got rid of those sandals and started wearing proper shirts and slacks and shoes. With my winnings today, I'm going to buy one of these little Fords to drive around in. Then I'll drive you around and buy you Champagne." Isabel reached over and patted Uki's thigh and hiccoughed.

Uki pulled over and stopped. Facing Isabel, he said, "I think you have had enough champagne for now."

"Did we run out of gas? How romantic." Isabel patted Uki's thigh again and winked.

"Why don't ya' hand over that bottle now so you have time to straighten up before we git home?"

"It's not empty yet!"

"That's ok." Uki reached over on the floor and freed up the bottle from between Isabel's feet.

"Whoa, boy, your movin' a little too fast for me. I'm 87 years old, and it takes me a while to warm up to a man now days. Maybe a couple more dates? What do you

think? Eighty-seven. I'm pretty sharp for 87.

102

But there's one thing I don't do anymore. I don't buy green bananas any-more. No, I don't." A big yawn stifled further conversation as Isabel sagged to the door side of her seat and drifted off.

The rest of the drive was quiet and uneventful. He drove Isabel to the entrance for assisted living. She was snoring lightly as Uki parked and went inside for assistance getting Isabel safely to her apartment and to her bed.

Back at his home, Norbert A. Toddle was on top of the world as he changed into his tuxedo for the reception. The keynote address was well received, and the following panel discussion generated many perceptive questions. *We are on the national map.* He chuckled (not something he had been raised to do, but this was an exceptional moment). Particularly the younger executives seemed interested. Norbert noted that the older he got, the younger the membership appeared. "A Case for Diversity in Senior Living" did not impress some of the patriarchs who find the status quo quite comfortable. Apparently, they had not yet been roused by falling occupancy numbers. *It will come knocking at their doors soon,* Norbert thought, as Drusilla tied his bow tie.

"What was your topic today, dear? You did tell me but it has slipped my mind."

"A Case for Diversity in Senior Living."

"What did you say about it?"

"That demographics and income limitations narrow the pool of potential incoming residents in our area to a group of culturally very similar affluent individuals. I suggested that diverse cultural exposure could enliven the mind and spirit leading to a better quality of life for all."

"How would you go about doing that? It seems like a major effort," said Drusilla with a satisfied smile as she patted the completed perfect bow.

"I would seek out ethnic and cultural groups willing to come and tell about their backgrounds with stories, photos and songs, and about their current lifestyles. Groups like the Seventh Day Adventists, the rabbis from the Shalom Temple, the pastors from the AE Emanuel Church, the priests from the new St. Patrick's church in Kennett Square, the Mormons from the new temple in South Philadelphia, possibly even a politician, although that may be going too far. They would be invited to spend the day in discussion groups and to stay for dinner. In the evening, we would all meet in the auditorium for a general discussion so that residents and guests could interact, expand their knowledge bases and become more comfortable with people of different backgrounds. We have empty apartments should any guests wish to stay over for a brunch the following day. Their meals would be the only expense. Hopefully some of the leaders might consider retiring here. Filling apartments with responsible residents is a priority right now."

From the bedroom window Norbert saw the

limousine pull up as he was putting on his tuxedo jacket and giving himself a last look in the mirror. "Ready, dear? Our driver is here."

Drusilla, in a classic royal blue evening gown, diamond broach on the left shoulder, a double strand pearl necklace and a silver bracelet on her wrist, was the very image of a grand dame if you can be one under the age 70 years. She swept into the limousine, felt and smelled the luxuriously soft leather upholstery and settled back. She imagined her entrance at The Union League and tried to recall who would be there to see her arrival in the Rolls Royce. She knew nothing about cars except to recognize luxury vehicles costing over $200,000.

"Claude, can you hear me?" She asked. "Please tell us about the limousine."

"Use the telephone in your arm rest, dear. Press down on that button to talk. Use a normal voice otherwise it will startle Claude. Release it to hear his reply," Norbert cautioned. "It belongs to Mr. and Mrs. Tanaka."

"Oh, yes, I see. Thank you." Drusilla marveled at Norbert's breath of knowledge - he even knows about automobile voice transmissions. "Pardon me, Claude, can you tell us about this automobile. How did the Tanaka's come to own it?"

"Yes Ma'am. It was custom built in 2012 for President Hugo Chavez of Venezuela. The year before his death."

"It is in beautiful condition, just like new. How did the Tanakas obtain it?"

"Mr. Tanaka and Shanti were in Venezuela with an NGO, Caritas, I believe, to help bring in medical supplies and food for the people. The country was on hard times and was selling off many holdings. Mr. Tanaka and Shanti felt a great sense responsibility to protect valuables and historic antiques from being damaged or lost. In line with that mission they bought this limousine at a government sale. They bought the Alfa Romeo sport coup at the same time along with other antiques from the palace."

"How do you know all this history?" asked Drusilla.

"Yes Ma'am. You see, I chauffeur high end vehicles professionally. When these purchases were made, I was contacted to escort them back to California. Excuse me, but we are passing City Hall and turning onto South Broad Street. We'll be at The Union League in a few minutes."

The Rolls eased to the curb in front of the French Renaissance brick and brown stone façade of the Union League, founded in 1862 as a gathering place for Philadelphia gentleman supporting the Union cause in the Civil War. The dramatic twin circular staircases were guarded by the Washington Grays monument and the Spirit of '61 National Guard statue. Claude collected Mr. Toddle then went around to open the curb-side rear door to assist Mrs. Toddle to the sidewalk.

Drusilla remarked, "Your posture and carriage are those of a military officer. Am I right that you spent considerable time in uniform?"

Claude hesitated for a moment then leaned down and spoke softly, "I *did time* in a uniform, but it was for carjacking truckloads of luxury cars into Mexico. Our little secret." He winked then announced, "I will be here for you when you wish to return home." Transferring Mrs. Toddle's arm to Mr. Toddle and with a sight head bow and a two-finger touch to the cap, Claude returned to the limousine. Drusilla gazed up at the historic building then ascended the staircase levitating between the real and the surreal.

Later that evening at home Drusilla recalled, "Norbert, dear, I meant to tell you. Ted Johnson was looking for you this noontime. I told him you were giving a lecture in center city and could not be reached."

"Ted's a township commissioner," yawned Norbert. "Remind me to call him from the office in the morning. Good night."

"I'll try. Good night, Dear."

CHAPTER 16   SENIOR SPORTS DAY

"Charles, we need new and better signs for Senior Sports Day. Look at these. The rain last year warped the cardboard." Eleanor dumped a stack on the center table of the small multipurpose, news office, ping pong, Wii bowling and events planning room. The residents have complained that they need more space for volunteer activities and sports noting that it was more the size of a voting booth.

"What we need even more is for other residents to volunteer to take charge of this project. We have been doing it for nine years, and I fervently wish some of the younger people would assume leadership," Charles sighed shaking his head as he sorted through the washboard signs. "Al Ladenhofer made these but both of his wrists are casted since the bicycle accident."

"Why was he riding a bike? I never did understand what happened."

"It was his bike, but he had not ridden it for years. He decided to clean it up and ride around the drive. Apparently, he was doing well and decided to try one of the walking trails. He hit a tree root and went over the handle bars, down a slope into briar bushes and broke both his wrists. He will be laid up for several weeks. Who else has the talent to make new signs? I cannot think of anyone can you, dear? Eleanor stopped and thought hard. She was very good at names and talents. When a full minute passed, Charles knew there was trouble.

"Prepare yourself, Charles. You are not going to like my one and only suggestion. He seems to overcome barriers and accomplish tasks with innate talent, through an array of contacts and gifts or through skullduggery. He does these things quickly – miraculously. Charles, I give you: Mr. Tanaka (Eleanor has never been able to utter 'Uki')."

"Ugh" Charles doubled over as if hit in the solar plexus. "No, there must be someone else. Really, how could you bring up his name?" What about Shirley Jansen-Johnson? She is an artist."

"She works exclusively with dogs and cats in tempura. You have to face it square on. There is no one else unless we look for an outside contractor and that would be prohibitively slow and expensive."

Deep thinking filled the air. Silence. More silence. Charles opened his mouth, raised his right index finger, closed his mouth and lowered his finger. Slowly he walked to the wall phone and paged the directory on the stand, turned, looked at Eleanor, sighed, turned back and dialed.

The CZX7000 lit up blaring out Chuck Berry's "Rollover Beethoven".

"Hola! Les."

"Yes, hello Mr…., ah Uki. We are setting up for the Senior Sports Day, and our signs warped in the rain last year. We were wondering if you know of a sign painter who would not be expensive and could initiate making new signs promptly."

"Right there."

"We are in the multipurpose room. It is hard to find…"

"Les, you are tracked. 5 minutes."

"He is coming now," Charles reported, hanging up the phone. "I hope we are not making a mistake."

"Amen to that," Eleanor affirmed, looking over last year's itinerary.

Pigtail, earth-tone brow band, faded rainbow pull-over half shirt, black knee-length shorts and sandals bust through the door. "Whatcha got?" Sifting through the pile of signs on the table, Uki chuckled, "Egg and spoon? Book head balance walking? Fans, I'll make signs, but these two gotta go! Mini golf - that's cool. Need more races. Show me where they go later. One week it'll be done. Kick back, I'll set up the new events." Uki was gone with the signs.

Charles and Eleanor looked at each other, eye brows up, mouth corners down.

"What have we unleashed?" Charles sighed.

***

Three weeks later, the morning after the big event, Charles looked up from the newspaper. "Eleanor, four weeks ago, Tanaka made those signs. Three days ago, he put them up. Yesterday was Senior Sports Day. Today we have a half a page of coverage in the *Daily Chronicle*. That is a first. It also may signal our last Sports Day. Listen to this:

Senior Sports Day. Mayhem at the Manor.

"At 9 A.M. the program began peacefully under blue skies, but at 11:13 A.M., midway through the final turn in the power chair race, a chair from Toddle Manor nudged a chair from Harrison Hollow causing the latter driver off the track, down an embankment and into the retaining pond. The driver, once back on dry land, apparently had colorful comments for the driver of the silver and black chair from Toddle Manor. Police and fire sirens interrupted further confrontation. There was a shouting and shoving match going on at the minigolf shelter. A Toddle Manor golfer was accused of cheating to win the tournament on the 18th hole. His hole-in-one reportedly was obtained by bunching up the tee pad and chipping the ball over the intervening plastic nesting Canada goose and alligator normally navigated on this par 3 hole. One team member was pushed backward falling through the golf shelter's screening, accidentally pulling the fire alarm which activated the sprinkler system and alerted the fire department. Brawlers were dispersed by the fire men whose axes made short work of the wooden shelter. Chief Martin Waller reportedly proclaimed, 'We won't see another fire in that building.'

"The Greenwood Village's Resident Council, on behalf of the Greenwood Gophers, has filed a formal complaint with the Toddle Manor's Toads citing unsportsmanlike conduct. They are demanding restitution for three bent putters, sundry stained and torn golf shirts and trousers and the winner's trophy – a dozen exploding golf balls.

"Norbert Toddle, owner/operator of Toddle Manor, could not be reached for comment. A statement from his office indicated that an inquiry was underway. One resident involved in the dispute spoke to us on the condition of anonymity.

"Q.: What is your reply to the charge of cheating at mini golf by altering the tee pad and shooting out of bounds?

"A.: Hey, dude cool it. Just playin' a game.

"Q.: But the rule says....

"A.: What rule? I don't dig rules. Rules are history – so yesterday. This is a fun time - no memorizing rules, man.

"Q.: Were instructions given before commencing play?

"A.: You still hung up on rules? Potty training tough on you?

"Q.: Do you believe that games should be played by the rules so that everyone has an equal chance of winning?

"A.: I'm buildin' peace and happiness for dudes like you. Buildin' a cool fun New Life Suites and Spa right here where you can forget rules and start livin' that good life. Do yourself a favor, take off the tie, kick back and unwind. Adios, amigo."

Charles' blank, pale face alarmed Eleanor. She rose, steadied herself and said, "I'll fix you a cup of tea."

Chapter 17 THE GRANT

Uki had been summoned to the Administrative office *immediately*. "Have you seen this morning's *Daily Chronicle*?" demanded Norbert Toddle as Uki slid into his usual leather chair. "You have single-handedly destroyed decades of carefully nurtured reputation! Why? What are you doing? Who do you think you are? What do you have to say for yourself?"

"Bert, ya' sure do get hot over nothin'. Cool it, man, chill. I got 14 tweets this mornin' sayin' 'sounds like a cool place, how do I sign up?' Toddle Manor is coming out of the ice age, Bert. We're startin' ta' rock. I like helpin' folks, and you sure need it. So just relax. The good times are rollin' in."

"You are driving me to distraction! Now listen to me, Mr. Tanaka, I am going to have you removed from Toddle Manor. We cannot and will not tolerate your destroying the Toddle name built up over three generations on this estate!" Uki quickly pressed several keys on the CZX7000. The private printer in Norbert's desk drawer whirred. Toddle flinched, looked about, opened the drawer and removed three pages. There were two black and white photos and a page of boldfaced printed text. The pictures were of racks of bottles and a close up of a bottle of Canadian Club Blended Whiskey.

The text said, "Senator Norbert Toddle, wealthy sugar king, was a bootlegger! Recently discovered were bottles of Canadian Club whiskey worth more than $250,000 found in a hidden cellar on the Estate. It seems the whiskey was smuggled over the border into the US from Windsor, Ontario, a common route during prohibition used by Al Capon and many others. It is not known yet how Toddle used the whiskey. Did he use it to influence his state senate campaigns of 1922 and 1926 directly or indirectly? Did he sell it to local speak-easies? Both were and are illegal practices. We will report on the new facts as they are uncovered."

"This is somethin' I knocked out just for your enjoyment. Hope ya' like it."

Toddle smirked, shook his head negatively, "What have you concocted now? This is ridiculous. I will sue you for slander. More reason for evicting you."

"Bert, let's walk down to the stables for a little 'show n' tell'."

Toddle frowned as he looked at Uki's poker face.

"Mr. Toddle?" came over the intercom.

"What is it, Rhonda?"

"There are three people in dark suits walking slowly across the south lawn. They seem to be looking around, talking to each other and taking notes."

"Ah ha! Thank you, Rhonda. I will follow up." Toddle smiled and looked directly at Uki, "Finally I am getting some action from the state after months of calls and letters complaining that the Manor was under-going unwelcome changes despite my resistance. Now I'm getting some serious action and I'm going to make the most of it. I will be speaking to you again, mark my words. Good day!"

Toddle straightened his tie as he strode through the lobby past the maroon velveteen lounge chairs, over the large oriental rug, around the grand staircase, past the silver tea service set on the Victorian table and across the Great Hall. He exited the French doors and briskly traversed the south patio.

Two men and a woman were at a worktable covered with blueprints, talking and pointing up at the rear of Toddle Manor. Uki knew they were coming and had set up the table before being summoned to the office. Mr. Toddle scanned the area for a state police car to take Uki away in handcuffs, but none was present. Not good. There was a *Daily Chronicle* news truck pulling in the service drive and parking in the staff parking area. Norbert Toddle shuddered, the smile faded; all news is bad

news even if it's good news. What have I done?
I just complained to the authorities and asked
for a cease and desist order. I don't need to
make a public example of a resident, that will
make enrollment even worse than it is now.

"Good morning lady and gentlemen," the
smiling, confident, square shouldered Toddle
welcomed. "I am Norbert Toddle, the owner
operator of Toddle Manor," he said trying not
to smirk as he eyed Uki easing in around the
corner of the building behind a Rhododendron
bush. "How may I help you?"

Residents and staff began gathering as news
personnel set up lights, cameras and sound
equipment. Toddle mused that it was just like
children hearing the good humor truck.

"Mr. Toddle, I am Lawrence White Chambers.
This is Theodore Winslow and Sylvia Whit-
Smythe Pakkhi-Wcykwuzki," nodding to his left
and his right. "We represent the Advancements
in Community Living section of the Hamilton,
Whithers, Kendall, Wcykwuzki and Golden
Foundation for Better Living in America. I am
sure you're aware of our philanthropic and
creative endeavors over the years."

Toddle was unable to respond other than a nod.
A shroud of doom replaced his hopes for
retribution. *Were these persons actually giving
approval to this travesty?* To gain time Toddle
stammered, "Where are your official

headquarters? I'm sure I've heard of you, but you are not local here are you? I mean, not East Coast?"

"Our headquarters are in Omaha Nebraska. We give financial support to break through and creative endeavors in community living throughout the United States. The East Coast until now has not provided creative ideas in this area. Therefore, we were delighted to read of your concept to bring together the great generation, the quiet generation and the generation of rebellion, peace and political correctness, alias the boomers, in cooperative community senior living. We are excited about this active encouragement of cultural intermingling in senior living. The time has come to implement cross-cultural communal living and efficiencies of energy and land use. The Foundation thanks you for this admirable initiative. The good people living here are showing vision, cooperativeness, open-heartedness and patriotism."

A stunned pause while some of the 83 souls, whose hearing was good enough to comprehend, simultaneously dropped their jaws and gasped, "What?"

Mr. Chambers continued, "Mr. Toddle, if you would please step over here where the microphones and the television cameras are set up I would like to continue with a few remarks on camera. Yes, that is good. Now a little closer together with Mr. Toddle in the center, thank you. Are you ready boys?"

"Boys and *girl*, Mr. Chambers."

"I beg your pardon. I couldn't really tell in those overalls and all the long hair. Are you all set? All right we're getting thumbs up to proceed."

"Mr. Toddle in recognition of your groundbreaking initiative of inter-generational cultural communal senior living as noted and aptly described in your grant application and in the accompanying newspaper articles and reviews, here in this lovely setting, on behalf of the Hamilton, Waters, Kendall, Wcykwuzki and Golden Foundation for Better Living in America, we wish to present you with this check for $500,000. This is the first installment of a three-year grant for construction, implementation and evaluation of a holistic program. Integral to this grant is an ongoing seminar program to be developed by you and scholars for the evaluation of process and outcomes with the goal of annual publication of these results. Presenting you with this giant reproduction of your first grant installment, we will pause for a moment for photo-graphs to be taken." Mr. Chambers reached over, found Toddle's limp right hand and shook it vigorously as he smiled into the cameras. "Would you care to address this body and the national audience that will be seeing this historic event on the evening news, Mr. Toddle?"

The size of the grant only served to further accelerate chaotic collision of cognitive fragments in Toddle's brain. In short, Norbert was flummoxed. He called upon every ounce of past training, family tradition, and studied behavior for such life-threatening circumstances.

"Ahem," (he could have used a glass of water) "I am, I am grateful and honored to accept this grant from your Foundation. I could not be more surprised. Thank you for your recognition of our forward thinking in this field of community compatibility living and our diligent and steadfast resolve to create a better world for seniors here and across the nation. The awarding of this grant will undoubtedly stimulate other communities to initiate similar projects. "We will not slacken in our resolve to advance this new era of peaceful, joyful, energy efficient, eco-friendly living. Again, with heartfelt thanks, I accept this check and the full grant."

The applause was very light to absent among the longtime residents but was vigorous from behind the Rhododendron bush.

Once the media and the dignitaries had driven off toward the city of Philadelphia, Uki stepped forward and gave Norbert a vigorous handshake, a big smile and tongue–in-cheek cheer, "Bert that was eloquent! I din't know you were so big on this project. Thought ya' were a little down on it. Shows how wrong I can be. With this grant, we'll kick inta' high gear. The blueprints er done. The architects er scheduled and the contractors er standing by. I meet with 'em at 1 P.M. Don't worry I'll handle the whole thing. Oh yeah, the New Life Suites and Spa has 75% occupancy commitment. Thought you'd dig that," he winked as he rolled up the blueprints and headed for his new trailer.

Norbert Toddle stood alone. He looked at the 3' x 5' check, looked at the Manor where he had been born and raised, at the trees and shrubs, at the lawn where he, little Norby, his older sisters and his much older brother had played, at the blue midmorning sky and then back to the check in his hands. He took a deep breath and slowly walked across the patio toward the French doors. *What grant? What news-paper articles? What reviews? And then there is the whiskey issue to investigate. Was grandfather a bootlegger? That could be a powder keg. Mr. Tanaka has a lot to answer for, Norbert thought angrily, but he had better proceed cautiously for the present. Norbert wondered if this were a good day or a bad day? One thing it certainly was not. It was not, "So generation."*

CHAPTER 18   THE VOTE

"This meeting of the Residents Council will come to order," Charles firmly stated as he brought down the gavel and seated himself at the front table.

"Old business:

Recurring complaint regarding the green beans. As background, I've asked our historian Alexander Alexander to review the history of this persistent complaint with the hope of adding perspective to help us resolve this issue with finality. Alexander please present your report"

"Ah, ah, wait a minute until I find my place. Oh yes, volume 1 page 1."

"How many pages do you have there?" interrupted Charles checking his silver engraved family pocket watch.

"Ah, in which volume?" Alexander asked looking over his half glasses.

"How many volumes are there?" Charles asked clearly concerned.

"Three so far but I'm just up to 1940."

"1940! Toddle Manor was a private residence in 1940. It opened its doors in 1948," Charles interjected becoming irritated.

"Yes, correct but I have family cook's journals that go back..."

"Alexander, your dedication to this task is very much appreciated, but could you summarize 'likes' and 'dislikes' in the last year and 4 years ago? That should be quite sufficient as a departure point," Charles firmly asserted.

"Residents liked the following: Last year: al dente (undercooked and crunchy) – 58. Overcooked and limp – 51.

Four years ago: al dente (undercooked and crunchy) – 20. Overcooked and limp - 113."

"Thank you, Alexander. It seems that there has been a clear trend toward people appreciating al dente over heavily steamed green beans. The beans, of course, are more nutritious when they have not been steamed until they are limp. Given that this is communal living and that we all are eating vegetables prepared in the same fashion, there will be residents who will need to make vegetable choices accordingly. There are a variety of options if we will be a bit flexible. I believe we have discussed green beans to the fullest over the years. Therefore, assuming that we all agree that there is no benefit in future discussions on the topic of green beans, I call for a vote in favor of ending green bean discussions with the conclusion that beans should be cooked al dente for better nutrition. Those in agreement raise your hands. All opposed? Scanning the responses, it appears rather close. Secretary, please count the votes for and against the measure. A simple majority rules."

Eager to move on, Charles launched into new business.

"New business: "Construction of a large new contemporary wing over the existing south patio and adjacent lawn.

"Mr. Toddle, always a considerate and caring gentleman, wisely states that he will not proceed with the construction without resident approval. We do live here, and we will be most affected by this travesty. Therefore, he has asked me to conduct a thorough discussion and a vote to determine how the majority of residents feel about said construction. If the majority are against the construction, Mr. Toddle states that he will return the grant, and the issue will be closed.

"Mr. Tanaka's clandestine effort to build a hippie commune on the south lawn of this historic and noble Manor is open for discussion.

To ensure that this discussion is totally neutral and non-prejudicial, I caution all those here against any hostile or pointedly aggressive remarks or any unseemly gestures directed at Mr. Tanaka regardless of how repulsed you may be by the very thought of such a venture."

Eleanor handed Charles a slip of paper. He rose slowly, "The vote count on the motion to end discussion of green beans has failed to pass by a vote of 53 yea and 57 no. The matter will be tabled for further consideration." *Over my dead body,* thought Charles.

"Continuing with new business, Toddle Manor has been subjected to unwanted news coverage through remarks made to reporters from the *Daily Chronicle* by an anonymous resident most assuredly Mr. Tanaka. Mr. Tanaka has requested an opportunity to address our membership to clarify his position. The chair recognizes Mr. Tanaka."

"Hey thanks, Les," Uki shouted out as he jogged up the center aisle. Shanti smiled and applauded.

"It's Mr. Chairman, Mr. Tanaka," corrected Charles.

"Cool, Chair," Uki smilingly obliged. He took the hand microphone from Charles, turned toward the resident audience and leaned against the

front table with his back to the officers. "I
wanna cut you in on a great venture that will
lower your monthly maintenance fees.
Whether we like it or not Boomers, like Shanti
an' me, 're turning 65 every day. 'Round here
they're mostly well-heeled and looking for the
next great thing. Kids are gone, or should be,
and it's time to downsize from the big family
house. But where ta' go? Where they gonna
get a cool life style? Well not at Toddle Manor.
This place is losing occupancy more every year.
It will go under sooner or later in your life times.
UNLESS (dramatic pause, hand in the air) unless
you good folks vote to let me add a cool New
Life Suites and Spa on the south patio and lawn.
Trust me, I know what they want, and they will
get their way somewhere else if not here. They,
I mean we, will buy up for cool comfort, fresh
air, exercise, healthy cuisine, fun, leisure stuff
and parties. We plan to live forever, never be
sick, debilitated or demented. There has to be
a life style to back that up. I will build it here.
You keep your conservative lives in the Manor;
that's fair. Do it but let the NLSS pay some of
your expenses. The upfront move-in payments
and the monthly maintenance fees will be
much, did I say 'much?' yes, much higher than
yours.

"All the monies will flow into the one pot. Y'a
get the idea? They pay more, you pay less.
Occasionally I get the feeling that a few of you
don't particularly like me or maybe not even
Shanti. A muffled 'yes' spread like diesel
exhaust across the auditorium. We come in and

out by an extension of the front drive around to south parking. We live facing the south lawn. You keep all that you like as is and live with the security that Toddle Manor 'll be on solid financial footing for the future. You'll be welcome to join in all of the new activities including swimming, tennis, bocce, meals at pool side and parties. Now is that cool or what? Who wants lower maintenance fees? Let's see some hands. Hey, Les, chair guy, look there, most everybody! It's even possible that you could be future investors. I'll give the word as we go along, but Toddle wanted the residents' input now. He'll sure be happy."

"The chair requests clarification. How is it that such a large facility, if it were ever to pass the township Board of Commissioners, would decrease maintenance fees for current residents?"

"That's cool, Les. New higher fees for these luxury suites, like I said, green construction, efficiencies of heating and cooling. Add on economies of scale in purchasing, full occupancy and you have it."

"We would need to see very specific financials before approving any such plan," countered Charles.

"Sit down, Charles, we need his generation to

move in here for us to survive," shouted Zak Ottoblurter.

"Order, order. Wait for the chair to recog..."

"I say give this Uki guy a chance. Remember he's the guy who bailed us out in grand style when the Atlantic City bus broke an axle. Look, this ship is leaking badly, neighbors. If anyone has a better idea, let's hear it now!"

"Zak, sit down. You are out of order! Are there any other comments? Yes, Gladys?"

"Well, I do not mind saying that I do not approve of Mr. Tanaka's dress, his style, if you can call it that, his slouchy ways, his pony tail, and I don't know where he gets all of his money. I do not appreciate the way he has upset our previously peaceful, proper and orderly lives. Furthermore, although she is pleasant enough, I object to the wife running around here half naked. However, my father always told me, 'Gladys, if someone wants to tickle your pocket nerve, think long and hard before you turn him down.' So with reservation, I say it is wise to agree with Zak. If Mr. Tanaka and his kind will keep the Manor solvent, then I can abide it. Over time most things do tend to become tolerable. Dinner served at pool side and lounge chairs with TV sets do sound attractive."

"Opinions noted. Now may I hear from some of the many opponents of this ridiculous proposal?" Charles scanned the residents furtively searching for a raised hand. "Speak right up. We need to hear from you. George? Shirley? Anyone? Anyone at all? Yes, Mary Lou."

"Well, Charles, I am not speaking 'against' but I would like to say that I enjoy the classes that Shanti gives. The Chi Gong exercises are nice, peaceful and restful. I like being with her and the other residents to do the exercises with. I wish the others would say something. I feel more fit and healthy, and the vegetarian diet is very good for me. I've lost 5 pounds. With swimming pools, there will be even more to do. So, I think that instead of just tolerating the Tanaka's proposal, I for one, will wel-come having more like-minded people to enjoy the fresh air and outdoor activities with. Thank you."

"Mary Lou, you ended two sentences with prepositions in the past 15 seconds. Your remarks are noted. Let me see the hands of all those opposed. Surely all of you are not reluctant to speak. Come now," entreated Charles.

"The Chair recognizes Zebedee."

"We've never done it that way before so, I'm against it."

"Good point. And who is that in the back? Isabel Larken? Yes, Isabel, do you wish to speak? Please stand so that we can hear you better."

"I remember that bus trip to Atlantic city and how the bus broke down. Well, it was Mr. Uki who came to our rescue. He thought about us being stranded and took matters into his own hands. He got some really good champagne. Now that's my kind of man; so I vote to do what he says."

"Yes, Zak."

"I move that we accept Uki Tanaka's proposal to build a New Life Suites and Spa on the south terrace"

"I doubt there will be a second to that motion."

"I second the motion," came from a chorus of voices.

"I call the question" Alexander Alexander called out. "Let's not waste time."

Reluctantly, Charles muttered, "The question has been called. All in favor say, 'Aye.'"

"Aye," thundered back. "Opposed say 'No.' I

repeat, those opposed say 'No.' The motion to call the question carried. Madam Secretary duly reread the motion to approve construction as proposed by Uki Tanaka."

It passed with overwhelming support. The murmurs now rose to a din. Chairs were pushed aside. Quickly Uki was surrounded by the inquisitive many. Charles looked about dejected, the gavel hanging loosely from his right hand.

Eleanor elbowed him, "Charles, close the meeting. Let's go home."

Mary Lou asked, "Uki, may I swim laps in your pool? I miss that here."

"Sure thing. Why don't ya' set up a schedule with our trainer, Wanda Thump. She'll be coordinating pool exercises and games."

"Can I get a vegetarian dinner at pool side?"

"Uki, what about water sports, like volley ball?" asked Zak.

"Will there be games like horseshoes, bocce, shuffle board?"

"What about art movies?"

Uki stood up on a chair and looking into the expectant faces of the group, he knew he had a winner. "The answer to all your questions is a big 'yes.' Shanti and me, we love ya' all and wanna see everyone have a good time just the way you like it, no rules. Just remember that means everyone, so ya' all have to live and let live. We're all different so give and take. I'll stay and answer questions as long as ya' want. Ya' gotta leave? Record your suggestions on my phone. I'll put it on the front table. Just say, 'Hey Uki' and it will record and 'Bye' at the end. Now who's next?"

Norbert Toddle stood gazing out the window behind his desk. The maple leaves were turning autumn rust to red, and the blue and white of the cloud-patched sky added to the glorious beauty of the season, but Toddle's mind was on MICE! Everyone has been complaining about the mice since the construction began two months ago. After the residents voted in favor of the new construction, the last nail was hammered into the coffin of hope to avoid this catastrophe from rolling over Toddle Manor. Worst of all, money had been the motive even for him! He could not blame Tanaka 100 percent. Oh yes, he had set it all in motion, but Toddle had to blame himself for looking at that big check in his office every day and feeling the rush of green fill his heart, his mind and his imagination. Greed! Shame! No, good business! Saving the Manor for everyone. A wise and selfless sacrifice for the general good. His father would have understood that, surely. Mice! Three weeks and no letup since the exterminators last attacked using all their weapons throughout the campus.

"Mr. Toddle, the Director's Forum starts in 5 minutes."

Toddle, jolted back into speaking mode, responded, "Thank you Rhonda, I am on my way." There was no way out of it. With a deep sigh, Toddle picked up his "Toddle Manor - Live with confidence" note pad and the family Mont Blanc pen, upgraded from ink fill to a ball point.

Once in the auditorium Toddle strode to the front and picked up the hand-held microphone from the polished mahogany family dining room table, now used for meetings. "Can you hear me?" Toddle said after flicking the switch on the microphone's handle. No one answered so he assumed it was on. "Thank you for coming to the Director's Forum this afternoon. It has come to my attention that there have been some complaints of mice recently. You will be pleased to know that that has been taken care of. We had Rodent Ridders place traps in strategic locations again three weeks ago. The effect of that action should have been noticed by now. We have been assured that there will be no further problem. My apologies for the inconvenience. We believe the problem was caused by digging the foundation for the swimming pools in the area of the south patio with field mice fleeing into The Manor. If you do happen to note a mouse in the future, please notify maintenance and they will assist you promptly. Thank you for your understanding."

"When will the mice stop running through my apartment?" asked a resident from the Lincoln wing.

A chorus of, "Mine too!" followed from Washington, Madison and Jefferson.

"When did you say the exterminators are going to come? It's getting worse every day? I even see them in the hall during the day!"

Mr. Toddle held up his hands. "Am I to understand that there is *still* a lingering problem? There should be no, and I emphasize the word *no*, problem by this time."

"They're everywhere!"

Uki stood up in the back of the room, "Bert, I have a solution and it won't cost ya' a cent."

"Mr. Tanaka, may I remind you for the 100th time, it is 'Mr. Toddle,' not Bert or anything else!"

"Yeah yeah, chill. You could use my help."

"You have 'helped' quite enough already. This whole construction enterprise has been your brainchild against my better judgment," Mr. Toddle said glaring at Uki as scarlet percolated up from his collar to his ear lobes. "I will contact Rodent Ridders today and have them return to completely redo the process. Thank you very much. The meeting is adjourned!" The executive director strode from the room.

Charles took Uki aside, "What on earth were you intending to suggest? Mr. Toddle was right, you know, you have caused a great deal of trouble here. I have to warn you that anymore 'good ideas' may put you in a very delicate position given your marginal popularity among residents and the administration! Personally, I have to say that if you sought residence elsewhere, it would not be disquieting."

"Les, you keep trudgin' the uptight trail, much as I've tried to help ya'. But don't quit on yourself. I feel that down deep inside there's a peaceful place. We just have to find it. Do you smoke?"

"What a silly question. It is not germane to the topic of your intrusiveness."

"It's relaxin'. You need somethin'."

"I discontinued cigarettes when discharged from the Army. That was a long time ago, and I have no desire to restart."

"Did it cut the stress?"

"Just a placebo effect, I presume, a distraction for a few moments."

"Let's go get some fresh air out back. Good for the mind, body and the spirit." Walking on the path toward the bench in the beech grove Uki asked, "Do you practice the peaceful three breaths?"

"Certainly not. What is that, some sort of witch craft?" Charles scowled.

"Part of peaceful livin'. Slow deep breath in, count ta' three, let it out slow and count to three before takin' the next breath in. Do it three times. Very relaxin', but ya' have to be concentratin' on the breath. Can't be thinkin' 'bout getting' laid or punchin' out some dude - just about the breath."

Charles turned sharply toward Uki, "Your vulgarity surpasses any possible virtue you may have. Really!"

Uki rolled a weed. "Have a smoke, Les."

"I do not smoke."

"Don't inhale. Ya' need to relax anyway ya' can. Here take this - it's my personal favorite. Take a puff. If it doesn't help, dump it."

"No, thank you."

"Have you ever stepped out of line?" Uki blew some smoke Charles' direction.

"I have done quite well playing by the rules," Charles replied.

They reached the bench in the beech grove and sat down. "Ya' ever wanted to bust out 'n have some crazy fun - let off steam?"

Charles did not wish to think about it. He had locked the door on that closet years ago and could not contemplate even peeking in. He shivered as memories of drunken fraternity parties and police raids leaked into his consciousness. He took a small puff.

"I have to check somthin'," Uki said turning on the CZX7000. Setting it on silent search, he whispered, "Mice out fast" and waited. Two seconds later, "Karl's Kats – 1.37 miles 8 minutes away. 30 kats by 7:00 PM today. Price negotiable/kat. Minimum six kats." Uki typed in a secure response, hit enter and signed off. He rose and turned to Charles, who had been tentatively puffing Uki's favorite, "How ya' feelin'?"

Charles dragged himself away from his image of standing on the bar singing, "47 bottles of beer on the wall, 47 bottles of beer," slowly blinked and solemnly declared, "Grammar books! Strunk and White, and Flesch, and Edward Johnson, and Dorothea Brande and Betty Schrampfer Azar are all melting away, swirling down, down, down a rat hole. Bah!" Another puff. "And do you know what?" Charles asked, looking at, but not clearly focusing on, Uki. "I do not give a dingdong. NO! Not a ding or a dong, ha, ha. Take that! I am sick and tired of hearing bad grammar – BAD GRAMMAR! Sick of correcting the perpinators, perpitaters. Thirty-two years teaching English and what did I accomplish? What? Nothing. Bad grammar is everywhere! Ahh! I am going to hold my ears and sing Tosca. Get away. Away. Bad grammar is everywhere." Charles rose, steadied himself and started toward Woodland Trail. "Away to the woods."

Uki called after him, "Les, are you relaxin'?"

Charles made a very slow half circle and peered at Uki, "My joints are so loose, my bones may fall apart."

"You're hangin' loose. Cool."

Tum. Tum tum. Tum. Tum tum. The sound drew Charles down the trail. Soft voices, "Ah wa - oh wa, inner spirit awaken to the drum."

Moving, flowing. Tum, tum tum. Into the circle. Vapor rising from the central urn. "Spirit rise with the vapor and the drum. Ah wa -oh wa" sang the chorus of vague naked figures circling, circling. Charles was in the vapor of lavender musk, floating in the vapor, swaying with the drum beat. Always tone deaf, Charles began to sing, "Ah wa - oh wa." He became a butterfly shedding the cocoon, wings opening tentatively then fully. "Free! I am flying, wa hoo!" Timelessly floating free. Unafraid.

***

"You, Uki?" the truck driver asked.

"Yeah, you Slade?"

"Dom. Slade owns the cats. I own the truck. Hundred cats - mean and hungry."

"Who is Karl?"

"Runs the operation out of Pensacola. Never met 'im. Where's the whiskey?"

"Easy, Dom," Uki said, finger to his lips as he looked about for other ears. "Guarantee me ya' can get 'em all back in the truck."

"Sure. Could be one or two runs into the woods, but they won't bother you. Feral cats live off the land."

"Mice are in the Manor from that construction over there," nodding toward the fenced off south patio and adjoining segment of lawn. "Cats will have to be inside and outside," explained Uki.

"Open all the doors. Attic too. Cats will find 'em. I'll back the truck up to 'em big doors next to the fencing. You open 'em up and stand back," Dom said. "And I'll be back in two days. Where's the whiskey?"

"Back up now, then the whiskey," said Uki firmly.

Dom looked at Uki piercingly, blinked and started the rust colored, formerly blue, '58 Ford 150's engine. At the French doors, the tail gate was dropped. Cats jumped, tumbled and rolled out as their cages were opened. They ran into the Manor, into the construction site, into the garden. Everywhere. Uki got in the truck and directed Dom to the parking space next to Uki's new trailer.

Uki produced two cases of Canadian Club. Dom loaded them in the truck bed, covered them with a moving pad and roped them down securely.

"Four cases. Need two more," Dom pronounced.

"Two more when you come back"

"Four cases now and you can keep the cats," bartered Dom.

"Two more cases when you take all the cats back. That was the deal. We don't want the cats. See you in two days." Uki slammed shut the tail gate and stepped back. As he watched the Ford curl up the side drive and over the rise at the Manor, Uki spoke into the CZX7000,

"Open ledger. Entry: Karl's Kats -#100 – 12 units now; 12 units later. Close ledger."

There was a sudden scream from the Manor, then another. The posters! Uki ran to the rear door of the trailer and pulled out a roll of 18"X 12" red poster paper with large black lettering and a box of stick pins. He locked the trailer and briskly walked up to the Manor. Uki rehearsed, "One poster for each floor of each wing, that's 8, then one each for the assisted living and medical units, one for the mail room." ALERT! PROFESSIONAL MOUSERS WILL BE ON THE GROUNDS FOR THE NEXT TWO DAYS. DO NOT ATTEMPT TO FEED, PET OR DISTURB THEM. THANK YOU. As Uki finish pinning up the mail room poster, rapid steps and bluster rapidly approached from behind.

"You! Well, who else? It is always you!" Mr. Toddle's eyes were protruding frightfully far out of his distorted red face. "Mr. Tanaka this is the last straw. What do you think you are doing?"

"Getting rid of the mice, protecting your image as the effective executive director. Just helping out a little where you are having trouble. Hey, two days the mice 'll be gone, and folks 'll love ya'. Take the credit, enjoy it. The Trust 'll pick up the tab," soothed Uki smiling benevolently.

Toddle blustered, blew and rocked up and down, back and forth. Finally, he got so blue that he had to inhale. With mouth still open, he pointed his finger at Uki and started shaking it, but no words came out. One long minute of this and Toddle suddenly stopped. "What trust?"

"The Toddle Trust for Senior Enhancement. You and I are the trustees. So far, I'm the only one using it, but you can any time ya' gotta worthy cause," offered Uki smiling brightly.

Toddle was still trying to separate fact from fiction. Almost afraid to ask, Norbert said, "What is in the trust?"

You never did check out the stable, did you? Do you want to see the ledger? I have it right here. Every bottle of Canadian Club is equal to one "unit." See here, today, Karl's Kats – total of 24 units."

Norbert closed his eyes, "I do not want to hear about this mythical trust and its mythical contents." He dropped his shoulders, focused on the poster and then on Uki again. He inhaled, raised his eyebrows, started to speak, shuttered, then turned and retreated to his office for two aspirin, water and thinking time – fleas, rabies, board of health. Pandora's Box would be open, and what if there really is a cache of bootleg whisky in the stable? The Board of Health would find that too! Mr. Toddle swiveled his chair and looked out the window hoping for a solution to rise from the reflecting pool or from the arborvitae just beyond. Closing his eyes, "Two days," he murmured, "Just two days." Suddenly he was very, very tired.

CHAPTER 20   THE GRAND OPENING

Mr. Toddle tapped the standing microphone. "If I may have your attention, please. Good afternoon one and all. Today we are pleased to welcome all of you residents-in-waiting to the official opening of the New Life Suites and Spa and all of our current residents joining together in this celebration. We are honored to have with us on the speaker's platform, from the Sylvania County Community Development Committee, Chairman, Mr. Hopewell Hayes-Hopper, and from the Advancements in Community Living section of the Hamilton, Whithers, Kendall, Wcykwuzki and Golden Foundation for Better Living in America that provided a generous grant making this building and program possible, with our grateful thanks, Ms. Sylvia Whit-Smythe Pakkhi-Wcykwuzki. Thank you for the applause. Such a beautiful May afternoon. One resident told me that the first week in May in southeastern Pennsylvania must be what heaven is like with the azaleas, geraniums, roses, dogwoods and magnolias all in bloom."

"The record shows that occupancy on move-in day tomorrow will be 100%. Welcome to all of you, our new neighbors. All of us here at Toddle Manor look forward to meeting, greeting and coming to know you. How exciting! We have arranged for food and music at stations here around the perimeter of the south lawn. Each one will welcome you with a different cultural theme reflecting and symbolizing cultural diversity.

"Now I would ask Mr. Hey-Hopper and Ms. Pakkhi-Wcykwuzki to join me here on the platform at the entrance to the New Life Suites and Spa to cut the red ribbon officially opening this green, ultramodern expansion to Toddle Manor."

As everyone gathered about the platform, Rhonda handed Toddle an oversized pair of shears. The featured three held the handles and cut the red ribbon to a great shout of joy flushing out a feral cat and two kittens from under the low platform. Cameras clicked and video cameras from the *Daily Chronicle* hummed as gold and silver balloons were released.

"Enjoy saying hello to the persons next to you. Tell them one or two sentences about yourself then reverse the telling and listen. Visit the booths with a new neighbor for music and cuisine. Guests on the speaker's platform please remain for more photos and interviews for the *Daily Chronical*."

Uki quickly stepped up on the platform. "Hey, more good news! Bert, I have an announcement. Hand me the microphone a minute."

"What are you trying to do?" muttered Toddle as he struggled with Uki over the microphone.

"Ya' gonna luv it, Bert." Pulling the microphone free, Uki pronounced, "The Toddle Trust for Senior Enhanced Living will provide $170,000 to build and maintain a rotunda and surrounding garden on the southwest lawn here." Uki pointed to a nearby space between the new pavilion and The Gardens assisted living. The facility will contain a library, solarium, an art studio and a reading room. In addition, the trust is sponsoring a monthly invited lecturer cultural series. The speakers will be selected by a committee of residents. I am making this announcement because Mr. Toddle is too shy and humble to tell you of his generosity. Let's have a big hand for Mr. Toddle!" After the hearty applause and the astonished Toddle's acknowledgement, Nobert looked for Uki, but he was nowhere to be seen. Grinding his teeth, Norbert boiled with the knowledge that he had been outmaneuvered again by this California hippy. This announcement ended his thoughts of trying to get rid of the whiskey, if it exists, before Uki could use it to embarrass him and the Toddle name. *How could his honored Grandfather have been a bootlegger? Well, that will be some soul searching for another day.*

As the group leisurely spread out over the lawn toward the perimeter green tents, the peaceful glow of sun and shade from the high canopy of oak, beech, sycamore and tulip poplar trees was shattered by raucous music. "You Ain't Nothin' But A Hound Dog." An 8-foot-high blow up of Elvis Presley and a 3-piece rock and roll combo on a red and purple festooned antique 1948 Chevrolet flatbed truck rounded the bend of the utility road. Complete with grill, coolers and party streamers, the truck stopped and parked on the south lawn. Spilling out of four cars, two with large rainbow-colored flags flying were super cool new residents, men with pony tails and beards; men and women in splash colored shirts, designer jeans, yoga pants and sandals. They were ready to rock. The Yuengling lager in coolers and the barbeque grill were off-loaded and set up to the big beat. The charcoal quickly glowed after a fire stick blast. Long tables, benches and chairs unfolded. Baskets of organic strawberries, oranges and Bing cherries were soon on the tables. "Don't You Step on My Blue Suede Shoes" played. Had to dance!

There was jumpin', twistin', jivin', swingin', shakin' and rockin.' Uki slid from the truck's cab singing and swingin'. He was soon joined by Shanti. The aroma of organic steaks, brats, turkey dogs and baked beans scented the air over the lawn which now was filled with dancing singles and couples from all the venues. "I'm All Shook Up."

The press quickly finished their interviews and

cameras turned to the dancers. Despite his exasperation at the disruption, Mr. Toddle walked his guests to the now nearly empty perimeter tents. There the colorfully dressed occupants gladly explained and offered samples of their specialty foods: African, Egyptian, Chinese, Israeli, Czech, Hungarian, Mexican and Cajun. Hearing the different music selections in the tents proved to be difficult over the combo's big rock speakers. After the press visited each venue, Toddle lead them and the guests indoors to tour the Manor and then to have dinner.

"That drum beat is starting to get on my nerves. It is 6 o'clock. I had hoped to have dinner in peace," Eleanor sighed.

"Well, the good news is that the music has been muffled by the new suites building," responded Charles as they started down the hall toward the dining room. Zebedee Chaladon, dressed in his usual black polo shirt and black khaki pants, was sitting on a high stool outside the dining room entrance. "Zebedee, what do you think of this new building and all this so-called music? Don't you think this is crazy?" asked Charles.

Thoughtfully nodding his head up and down, "Crazy, yes. We're here, because we're not all there."

Eleanor pursed her lips, laid a forefinger to her chin. "A deep thought, Zebedee; one I shall ponder."

After his guests had gone, Mr. Toddle sat alone in his office. The conflict raged. What to say and do about Uki's interference? He thought, should I call out Tanaka for his gross over-reaching or just to be thankful that the new building was proving to be the financial success he needed. Even *Manor* apartments were filling with people on the waiting list for New Life units.

What did Tanaka mean by interfering with a lovely planned reception exemplifying the grant's diversity mandate! He connected me with spending from a trust I have never seen or agreed to, he embarrassed me in front of important guests, and he ruined an expensive international food tasting of exceptional quality. A great deal of time and effort had gone into the planning, and he shows up with a truck, tasteless loud music and tailgate food. Disgusting!

Cool it, Bert. The trust? You got big kudos, man. Enjoy it. The party? What did they jump for? If your idea was so good, how come everyone came over for brats and beer and danced all over the lawn? I'd say my guys knew what the customers wanted. Next time, ya' need to check with me before going over the edge like that. Looks nice but outta touch. Thought you'd learned that by now.

Mr. Toddle could just imagine how Tanaka would roll that out slowly to make it jab deeply.

Norbert bit his lip, rose from his desk, closed his lap top, muttered, "Money in the bank," and headed for home.

That evening, Uki reviewed his ledger: Rotunda
— 8500 units to the builder.

Truck, tables, benches, grills, rock and roll combo, food, beer,

Elvis; all-in-all totaled 200 units.

Worth it, he thought, rubbing his feet. He had not danced that much for years. Shanti was hard to keep up with; she danced him into the ground and a couple other dudes too.

"Thank you for coming to the meeting today. You, our residents, and our loyal staff all have been through a great deal this past two years. Quite dramatic changes I must say. The noise, the disruption of our peaceful regularity, and the inconvenience of construction on the south lawn happily have ceased. The good news is that since the ribbon cutting ceremonies two months ago, the New Life Suites and Spa has had 97 residents move in. That is 100% occupancy." (Modest applause).

"A few of our established residents were opposed to the concept and to the construct-ion. However, with awareness of the need for broader participation in the society and community, most of you embraced the project for which I heartily thank you. I knew you would welcome our new arrivals with the same open-hearted friendliness and congeniality that you exhibit among yourselves and to guests. As always, we attempt to be in the forefront of our industry. With all modesty, I can say that we are the first in the northeast and mid- Atlantic regions to embrace this agenda for senior living. And as you know we have been the recipient of national attention and a special grant in recognition for our efforts.

In appreciation of your long suffering and

patience, I hereby announce that next month Manor residents will not be charged for meals except for guests. (Thunderous applause whistles and hoots). This is possible because of a onetime surplus generated by the New Life Suites move-ins." And again, thank you for your good humor, patience and cooperation. Are there any questions?"

"Yes, Mr. Werthen."

"There is a rumor circulating that you intend to build cottages at the perimeter on the south lawn. Is that a fact?"

"There is no plan to construct cottages on the south lawn. Environmental survey, township permits, green space regulations all would have to be satisfied before a capital campaign would be mounted for construction costs. However, if in the future there were a definite demand for cottages, consideration would be given to that possibility.

Another question? In the back - Mrs. Spreckle."

"When are we going to get green beans that are cooked? They are raw! "

"Here, here," from hoarse cries and accompanying foot stomping.

"Mrs. Spreckle, the chef carefully monitors the preparation of the green beans. They are cooked to the most nutritious and palatable state – 'al dente'– tender but firm. This method retains all the vitamins and healthful nutrients, don't you see?

Now are there any other questions about the New Life center or …."

"They are RAW and I hate them. Cook the beans!"

Others pick up the chant: "Cook the beans! Cook the beans! Cook the beans!"

"Quiet, please. Quiet; quiet, PLEASE! All right, please hear me out. You now have a food committee chaired by Mrs. Tanaka. Take this up at their next meeting. Our culinary director, Mr. Stuffsom will be present, and I am sure some agreeable accommodation can be achieved. If there are no more questions on the New Life Suites, then the meeting is adjourned."

Mr. Toddle turned and exited the nearby rear door patting his forehead with a monogramed linen handkerchief. As Charles Werthen exited the meeting, Toddle motioned to him. As they walked toward the great room, Toddle asked, "Mr. Werthen, I will be away for a few days on a speaking tour. This healthy mixing concept has grown and is keeping me quite busy. In my absence, would you be willing to be my resident intermediary? Rhonda is very capable of handling calls and of screening for forwarding to me those of importance. As president of the resident council, would you be available to advise her should a resident issue arise?"

"I would be pleased to assist appropriately as you request."

"Fine, thank you. I will let you know the times of my going and returning. It will be three days next week."

"Cook the beans! Cook the beans! Cook the beans!"

Toddle and Werthen ducked into the small lounge off the Great Room as eight residents marched through heading for the Madison wing door to the grounds.

"They will be circling the building if they follow their usual route. Could you be at the Food Council meeting next week? I will alert Jeff Stuffsom that the 'limp bean' brigade is on the war path again."

"Certainly," assured Charles.

"Is that another cat at the French doors? And

kittens to boot! I thought we finally were rid of them! That's the result of another one of Mr. Tanaka's ideas."

"Yes, but really you have to admit that overall, Toddle Manor once again has a firm financial base, there are no mice and both the Manor and you have gained national reputations," offered Charles.

"Yes, true. You are right. It is easy to forget the larger good in a moment of pique. I should be thankful, as hard as that is to admit. Well, thank you for helping out in my absence. I will be in touch before my departure. Do have a nice day."

EPILOGUE

Norbert Toddle balanced his national speaking and conference schedule with managing Toddle Manor and New Life Suites and Spa with the help of Ronda, now vice president for marketing and sales. Rhonda's salary raises and performance bonuses have brought about changes. She lost 15 lbs. working out at the "Y," switched from canned beans to gourmet grab-an'-go dinners and from Coors light to chardonnay and she has joined the on-line "Knock'em Dead" dating service. Gladys Hardwood, now vice president for protocol, has found her rightful place and does not let anyone forget it. Uki and Shanti have moved to the Ambassador Suite on the 3rd floor of the New Life Suites. They share the administration of the New Life Suites and Spa, assisted by Martha Olso, and have a smooth coordinated operation. Marylou Doceal assists Shanti with the naturist woodland walks, Chi Gong and meditation circles. Culinary Director, Jeff Stuffsom has moved on. He owns and operates "Naturale," a vegetarian restaurant in Philadelphia with financial backing from Shanti and Uki. Bud Peal, former head chef at the Manor, has replaced Stuffsom as culinary director and features a full vegetarian menu and green beans to order.

Uki spends several weeks Spring and Fall

managing a Kingsley Conn 4000-acre ranch in Oregon. He supervises the marketing, sales, planting, harvesting and shipping of his popular hybrid marijuana leaves, *cannabis toddleii highridgeii*, to wholesalers throughout the United States.

Thanks to Uki and Kingsley Conn's having at least one lobbyist in every one of the 50 states, marijuana sales for medical and recreational use are being legalized progressively throughout the country. This ranch, one of the 14 Conn-Cann ranches throughout the United States, Mexico and South America, was Uki's reward for negotiating the real estate purchases and for success in Pennsylvania, a tough commonwealth for marijuana legalization. He has a life time franchise. His share of the profits in a good year is in the range of $20 million. Over time that accumulation of cash will be enough to pay off any old California partner or creditor who might yet track him down.

Uki had made a fortune selling overvalued houses and mortgaged-backed securities and was well known in San Francisco and throughout California especially in the real estate and hedge fund circles. By April, 2007 he recognized that the good times were coming to an end soon. He sold out to his partners for top dollar. They could not understand why Uki wanted out of such a bonanza. Anticipating that there would be blow back on some hedge funds and housing sales, he and his life partner since their hippy days at Woodstock, Alice

159

Karowski of Scranton, Pa, moved to the outskirts of Chapala, Mexico over the Cinco de Mayo weekend.

Uki, never leaving an opportunity unexploited, contacted his *most* wealthy billionaire client, Kingsley Conn for whom he had purchased large tracts of land in the southwest for the development of "Golden West" retirement ranch communities. Uki let Conn know that he was now a free agent for "projects of interest." Reverting to their comfortable life style and to better cover their tracks, Uki and Shanti shed the San Francisco business, social and theater attire. They revived their hippie persona; long hair, bare feet, loose linen and denim clothes showing the old tattoos, and they practiced naturism whenever possible. Within a year, the call came from Kingsley Conn to assist in building up marijuana markets throughout the United States. Uki and Shanti had their pick of several states. They chose Pennsylvania. Shanti has expanded her talents. Now she writes a column called, "Uncover Nature" for *Naturist* magazine and is one of their staff photographers. Her mind, body and spirit mediation and Chi Gong exercise programs have grown into a franchise throughout the mid-Atlantic region. Her vegetarian courses and demonstrations add to her schedule. The new Life Suites and Spa division of Toddle Manor continues to thrive. There is a now nearly a three-year waiting list and planning has begun for construction of cottages at the fringes of the south lawn.

Shanti, Uki and Rhonda are an effective team. When Uki is in Oregon, they sync via teleconferencing every Friday at 4:30 PM ET. All these activities keep Shanti in Toddle Manor 11 months a year. She does fly out to the ranch for two weeks in the spring and fall to be with Uki. She visits her brother in Scranton on Halloween when her attire and tattoos are more acceptable.

It is a demanding life, but at the ranch, sitting back in their wicker rockers on the veranda smoking love weed and sipping gluten free vodka, they watch the sun go down over the Rogue River Valley. They smile, nod and agree that it couldn't get much better.

The next day as they were relaxing in first class seats on the nonstop flight home to Philadelphia and Toddle Manor, Shanti leaned over to Uki and whispered, "Lover, has anyone guessed that you are the much older Toddle son who ran away from Valley Forge Military Academy?"

Uki looks over at Shanti with a knowing smile and a low satisfied chuckle, "Nobody, love, not even good baby brother Norby." Uki recalled those years and his father's tirade.

"Rutherford, you what? You quit the Academy three months ago because you did not like the discipline? All of life is discipline! This is the last

straw. Rutherford, you have been a thorn in my side since you were ten years old. You are always getting into trouble. You were expelled from Country Day School and then from Exeter Academy. Arrested twice for smoking pot and four times for underage drinking and DWI's! I thought VFMA would make a man of you. Why couldn't you be a credit to the family? Why can't you straighten up and maintain our family's otherwise impeccable community and statewide reputation? I warned you when I bailed you out of jail the last time and got you into VFMA that I would disown you and never let you back in this house again if you failed to carry through and graduate with good grades and good conduct. I am a man of my word. Rutherford, I banish you from this family and from this Manor. We will never again speak your name. Get your things. Out you go, now! Goodbye and good riddance!"

My three-piece double breasted and mustached father would roll over in his grave if he knew I was back in the Manor and there to stay.

With a fist pump, "Gotcha!"

"What's that, lover?" Shanti asked.

"Nothin', sweet. Just reminiscin'."

47286428R00089

Made in the USA
Columbia, SC
30 December 2018